Tears for a King

Ron Rendleman

Jeremy Books
5624 Lincoln Drive, Edina, Minnesota 55436

5624 Lincoln Drive Edina, Minnesota 55436

Tears for a King

Copyright © 1979 Jeremy Books. All rights reserved.

Library of Congress Catalog Card Number 79-84295
ISBN 0-89877-003-3

No part of this book may be reproduced in any form, except for the inclusion of brief quotations in a review, without permission in writing from the publisher.

Printed in the United States of America

ACKNOWLEDGMENT

I am grateful to Lud Golz, Jerry Jenkins, Jim Johnson and others for their encouragement through the years of working on this book and to the various typists, especially Martha Kalter, Rita Schoenthal and Teresa Andersen, whose labor of love far exceeded the compensation.

"Niggerdemos" story on page 80 reprinted from LAY MY BURDEN DOWN, edited by B. A. Botkin. Copyright 1945 by the University of Chicago

PREFACE

Shocking, brutal, but true, *Tears for a King* is based on actual reports of doctors and other eyewitnesses who served on slaver ships and plantations in the mid-1800's.

This is not only a story of how men became slaves. It also tells how one slave became a man!

Chapter One

The bone-white beach blazed beneath the African sun. Nine crewmen from the Zong sprawled in the shade of a giant frond and listened to the Koromantyn war drums growing steadily louder.

Hour after hour they waited, fidgeting, drinking rum and telling tales. Cursing the heat and the giant flies, they told each other of the fortune they hoped to make and spend. When night finally came, they lay back and sleeplessly watched the meteors shoot across the brilliant tropical sky.

At dawn, the advance guard of the Koromantyns emerged from the jungle, followed by the slave caravan, a mammoth black snake creeping slowly across the white beach: men, women, and children force-marched by warriors armed with muskets and spears. Most of the captive men had five-foot tree yokes lashed to their necks. The yokes were supported on the shoulders of the men next in line. When the caravan was halted, many of the women and children collapsed on the sand.

Immediately, the Zong's crew began their work. Each man was professional and quick, sure of his assignment. The doctor was the first to deal with each slave closely, examining the eyes, ears, and hair. The second mate tabulated each person by sex and approximate age, while a third crewman, assisted by two others, branded each slave between the shoulder blades with a hot iron. The last man in line, Captain Albright, watched for any unnoticed signs of disease or unworthiness. At the same time he looked for a wench who might make the hot nights of the middle passage bearable.

Mongo stood in line and sullenly studied the proceedings. Covered with dust and caked blood, especially where the tree dug into his neck, he stood tall, massive, and, except for a loincloth, naked. Each time iron scorched flesh, his eyes flashed defiantly, his mouth hardened, and his hands tightened on the ends of the yoke.

The line moved slowly forward till the small boy just ahead of Mongo shrank back in fear of the iron and was beaten severely. Mongo exploded. Screaming in Ashantee, he split his yoke in two with one violent tug and lunged at the whites. He knocked down the nearest sailor with part of the tree and turned the hot coals over on him. He grabbed the man holding the iron, shoved him against a frond tree, and, jamming his forearm against his throat, forced the arm holding the iron up so that the man branded himself in the forehead. As the man screamed helplessly, the iron continued to burn flesh until six crewmen smashed Mongo senseless with rifle butts and marlinspikes. Some of the slaves in line had broken loose to help Mongo, but they were quickly overpowered by the armed Koromantyns.

Mongo's hands and legs were chained, and he was thrown into the long boat and taken out with the others to the slaver anchored beyond the reef. When the work was finished, the Koromantyn king was paid fifty barrels of rum and tobacco, and the crew returned to the Zong.

When Captain Albright climbed on deck, the first mate made his report. "Capt'n, I see's we're running tight, so I told ole' whiskers not to lay 'em down this trip, but to stow 'em sittin' up, tight 'tween each other's legs. Right Capt'n?"

The captain frowned. "Can't be helped. We'll lose some, but we'll be ahead in the long run."

"Aye, Capt'n, but I had to lay it on a few. That big Ashantee got 'em all worked up."

"Don't surprise me none. I saw it from what he did on the beach. Take some to break him." The captain walked aft to the slave hold. He paused and drank long from a flask of rum to fight the stench coming from the hold. Taking a lantern from the overseer, he stepped down three steps and looked into the blackness. A sea of terror-filled white eyes peered at him. To avoid detection by blockade patrols, the slave deck had been laid just twenty-six inches below the main deck. This forced the men to sit with their chins forced against their chests. The hold was built to store three hundred, but now it held four hundred and sixty. The women and children were put forward under the forecastle.

He heard the gasping of those farther from the hatches and knew that before long some would suffocate to death. At one time it might have bothered him. Now they were only stock, like so many hogs or mules.

Satisfied that the first mate had done his job, he climbed to the deck. The surgeon and boatswain were waiting for him. "Got room for these buggers, Capt'n?" the boatswain asked, nodding to the last boatload of blacks who had just come aboard.

"Wedge 'em in," the captain said through long gulps of fresh air. The boatswain began shouting orders, and the blacks were forced and whipped into the hold. The cries of anguish from those below rang out as they were packed together even tighter.

"Bosun, pipe all hands! Mister, give your orders to get under way!" the captain bellowed. He turned to the surgeon. "Doctor Bass, would you join me in my quarters?"

The first mate moved back and forth amidships shouting his orders. The men came out of the hold like ants pouring out of an ant hill, climbing aloft, or pulling on manila bunt, leech, and clew lines. The anchor was hove to the pipe with a seaman's chant; the sails began to blossom out, and the slaver moved off with her head westward. Her destination: Havana. Since she was one of the fastest Guineamen afloat, she would make the passage from the disease-infested port of Rio Pongo on the west coast of Africa to Havana in several months. The date: October 13, 1858.

Chapter Two

Captain Albright went to the bulkhead cabinet, took a bottle of choice Jamaican rum, and poured two drams each into two mugs.

"Swill away, man. It'll take the taste of the black heathen from your mouth." He threw down the drink and poured another.

Doctor Sam Bass picked up his mug, studied it a moment, then sipped it slowly.

"I keep forgettin' you're not a drinkin' man," the captain smirked. "In this business it can save your life." The captain was fortyish, obese, and red-faced, with tiny, slit-like eyes. He denied the fact that his grandmother had been an oriental.

The young doctor smiled. He was exhausted from the day's work. His lean face was covered with dust that had been streaked by tiny streams of sweat. His long, sun-burnt hair was disheveled, and his white gentleman's shirt was spotted with dried blood. He was not big, but the hands that played with the mug were broad and not typical of a surgeon's. The forearms, bare to the elbow, were well-developed. He looked up, amused. "Save my life, Captain? How?"

"Well, Lad, you won't find it in those fancy books of yours, but rum is a natural protector against plagues."

"I've never heard that," the doctor said, skeptically.

"Well, by jiminy, then consider this a good lesson. Never fail to do it before you go into the hold. It takes the stench and badness from your throat, swabs it clean. 'Nother thing. Always wear a camphor bag around your neck, and git into the habit of an Irish twist in your cheek."

"I see," the doctor said, half to himself.

The captain studied the young man sitting across the large oak table. The surgeon's papers said he was twenty-seven, but he looked younger. All during the voyage from Baltimore the man had kept to himself. He had proved himself able enough as a surgeon when he had amputated a sailor's mangled hand. The captain liked the man, but his independence bothered him.

"Doc," he said more amiably, pouring himself another drink, "you've had a good look at your first black devils. What do you think?"

Doctor Bass rested his mug on the table. "I found evidence of smallpox in some. I rejected them."

"Aye. When I saw the first one, I took a scare, I don't mind saying. I've seen the pox wipe out a whole ship, crew and all. If we got 'em all, we got a chance; but I don't like it. But, Doc, I was referring to the general nature of the beast. Your long face has me troubled. I told you when you signed on in Baltimore it weren't no picnic. Now, didn't I?"

Doctor Bass studied the captain thoughtfully. "Just

before we came aboard I saw men digging graves on the beach for a dozen decapitated bodies, the same poor souls I rejected."

"Aye, I gave the order myself."

"Why?"

The captain smiled. "You're surely familiar with the pox. Would you have them sent back to corrupt the entire coast? I tell you it can't be helped. It's a nasty business sometimes to an outsider, this ebony business. But a business it still is, Laddie. Never forget it."

"But to kill them? These people aren't animals!" the surgeon said angrily.

"Calm down, now! Your rough tongue don't set well here. There's a lot you haven't learned about the Guinea trade. In time things will be clear. You signed on for experience, and experience you'll get. We'll talk more. But now, I'd suggest you go below and look at the crewman that was burned by that Ashantee."

Doctor Bass knew it was useless to press the matter, and he silently withdrew. He made his way to the quarterdeck just as eight bells sounded for the change of watch. A stiff breeze had come up from landward and was blowing west. He breathed deeply to clear his head of the rum and thought he could smell the African violets he saw growing in the shady places while on shore. Africa had caught him completely by surprise. He was struck by the immense size and prolific abundance of plant life: leaves that could hide a man! Giant mangrove trees, standing majestic, yet almost choked by trailing networks of vines and flowers, humbled him, while colors, shades and hues he had never known before mesmerized him. He gazed at the rapidly receding shoreline. A melancholy color, purple. His thoughts returned to the suffering he had seen that day. He wondered if Africa was a purple land because it was a land of suffering.

It was hard to understand how such beauty could coexist with the ugliness of the slave trade. He had seen men dealt with cruelly before, but what he had seen today made him ashamed. He thought of the burned man in sick bay, felt guilty for having lingered, and started below. He passed close to the grated hatchways amidship and heard moans and a curious hissing. The first mate passed him.

"Bojo, what is the hissing sound I hear below from the hold?"

" 'Tis the savages, sir. Some of 'em's findin' it hard to breathe."

"Is there nothing to be done?"

" 'Fraid not. Packed in like herring what does it."

"Can't the hatchways be opened?"

"Too dangerous. Capt'n never allow it."

The young surgeon turned and looked long at the African coast line, then went below.

Down in the slave hold, Mongo sat with chin forced hard against his chest. His arms were chained behind him. Because of his great size, this position was more painful for Mongo than for most. His neck and shoulder muscles were stretched to the tearing point. Every so often he spoke to the man who was chained to him at the ankle; and the whole line shifted sideways, and he was able to raise his head some. But then the people on the end would soon complain, and it would be time to move to the left and work out the pain from that angle.

Always there was the maddening groaning and gasping for air and the death chant of the defeated. At first, there had been many questions which, as a leader, Mongo had tried to answer; but when they saw that he was as ignorant of their future as they, they returned to their misery and the death chant.

The women behind the wall chanted; and when Mongo discerned Tilah's shrill voice, he thanked the gods for protecting her from the *buckra*. And while the chanting and sobbing continued all through the night, Mongo prayed for strength and for his two little boys who were last seen running into the bush to escape the war men. He prayed that someone would find and care for them. He vowed that someday he would find his way back to them.

Just before dawn, the man next to Mongo began struggling violently; and he felt the warm liquid gushing on his arm. Too late, he realized the man had succeeded in ripping open his own jugular vein with his claw-like fingernails.

Chapter Three

The Zong moved steadily westward through the night at about eight knots an hour. By dawn she was 125 miles northwest of Rio Pongo and still running before a brisk breeze that blossomed her two masts of full-rigged sails. Built along clipper lines, she had been designed for one purpose: to carry black men as fast as possible from Africa to the slave markets in the Indies, South and North America. She measured 89 feet from stem to stern; and her depth in hold was only 8 feet, 5 inches. She had once done 16 knots during a squall; but with a full cargo, 12 to 14 knots was a safe running-to speed.

She carried 170 casks of water, enough for one pint a day for each crewman and slave, and some to spare. She carried 50 barrels of horse beans and farina for the slaves, and 10 barrels of yams, rice, and beef for the crew. These were her only stores. For armament, she carried two 12-pound carronades, one starboard, one port. Both were swivel-mounted to cover the widest possible view.

The 24 crewmen slept forward in the forecastle in hammocks which were taken down during the day to make room for the meals. The Zong's crew was typical of most slavers': rough, courageous, but at the same time fearful and superstitious of sea demons and what not; loyal to no country or man, but slaves to gold; happy-go-lucky, hardy professionals; and of varied nationalities. Bojo, the first mate, was a Greek and had lived at sea from the age of fifteen. He knew every port in the world and was feared and respected as the best and cruelest first mate in the trade. He was also thought to be the richest.

Sarpo, the second mate, was an Englishman. Originally a regular on the San Francisco to Hong Kong tea run, he had jumped ship in Honolulu after meeting up with a pretty Filipino girl. He had abandoned her and gone back to the states, only to become drunk in Baltimore and be shanghied aboard a Guineaman. He had deserted in Havana, only to be kidnapped again to sober up aboard the Zong.

On the first morning at sea, when the sun was a half golden ball on the horizon, all hands were piped to the deck to clear between fore and mainmast. A rope was fastened on four sides to form a large pen.

"Better load the carronades with partridge, Bojo," the captain ordered from the quarter deck.

"Aye, Capt'n," the first mate answered and turned to two men working near. "Mondock, you and Wulliver take a man each and tend to the long guns. Keep a sharp look-see. These black heathen are apt to do anything first time up. If so much as an arm is raised, fire away. The rest of you men . . . prepare yourselves!"

Since only the officers aboard the Zong were allowed to have firearms, the crew armed themselves with their own weapons. Fish-gigs, bolus knives, and marlinspikes began to appear as the men formed a circle around the roped-in pen. When they were all in position, the mate looked up at the captain.

"We're ready, sir," he called.

"Open the forehatch, then," the captain said. The heavy gratings were swung back, and the captives were brought up in pairs, their naked, perspiring skins shining as onyx in the bright morning sun. They needed no persuading, but stumbled out on deck, squinting from the brightness, uncertain, hunched over, unused to the chains, falling over themselves. Some were bloody, and some were near expiring; but they were all relieved to be breathing easily again.

Approximately half the hold were let up, men and women. Several of the women were pregnant and needed help to climb the steps.

"Mister, what's your count?" the captain thundered.

The first mate was climbing out of the hold. "Twenty-three dead, Capt'n. Should we heave 'em?" Crewmen were cutting the shackles off the dead and carrying them on deck.

"Not 'til the surgeon's seen 'em."

Doctor Bass was already examing the dead. Meanwhile, the farina was brought out in large kettles. Some slaves put their hands into the boiling hot porridge and gulped it down, while others ignored it completely. Mongo's wrist chains were removed so he could eat. Tilah found him, and they sat close together. When the water was given out, Mongo gave her his portion. He was thankful that she seemed to be well; she was so fragile. He whispered reassuring words to her.

"Some won't eat, Capt'n," the first mate yelled. "Should I invite 'em special-like?" His pocked-marked face twisted into a sneer.

"Nay, let 'em be. If they don't hunger by the morrow, we'll see."

The surgeon joined the captain on the quarter-deck.

"What did you find?" asked the captain.

"Eighteen dead from suffocation, five from self-inflicted wounds."

"Any signs of the pox?"

"No sir."

When the slaves had eaten, the mate began cracking his whip and shouting in native dialect for them to jump up in time to a marlinspike beating against a washpan.

Mongo and Tilah did not move till the whip cut painfully into their backs. Mongo saw the welts form on Tilah's back and spat curses at the mate.

The doctor and captain watched intently from the quarter-deck. After awhile the captain said, "You see, Doc, I'm not completely ignorant of medicine. 'Preventive medicine' I calls it. Exercise puts spirit back into 'em."

"Exercise will help them, but it seems many of them are either too sick or melancholy to do it."

"Aye, so it appears. Bojo, lay that cat on," the captain yelled. "Any drops out, pull 'im to the side an' give 'im ten extras for future thought."

The beat was increased. The sound of many chains clanging against oak vibrated through the ship as the mate's heavy whip lashed out viciously; and the screams of pain from the sweating, panting, bleeding immigrants from a great land became one long cry for mercy.

Tilah dropped to the deck. Mongo bent over quickly, scooped her up and supported her against him, all the time still jumping. He held her tight; and the mate, seeing them too close, raised the cat and struck them.

"Drop her, you black dog, or I'll whip you to a pulp," he shrieked between blows.

Mongo's leap was explosive, concise. The surprised mate landed on his back, Mongo on top of him. Three seamen swung their clubs, and Mongo's body fell limp. Bojo got up slowly, quite shaken.

"By God, he almost had me," he said, gasping and holding his bleeding throat. "Fetch me a line," he yelled. "Get the rest of 'em back, lay it into 'em." He picked up the whip and cracked it again and again at the black bodies.

The captain had come down to the main deck.

"Same one causin' all the fuss, Capt'n. He just about had me, he did. Tried to chew out my jugular. Beggin' your permission to hang 'im from the main top for the rest to see while the mem'ry's hot?"

"Finish him for good?" the captain asked, looking down at the unconscious giant at his feet. Mongo seemed even bigger aboard than on shore. The captain was struck by his muscular definition and noble features.

"Nay, man, he'll bring six hundred pieces," he said.

"But still, we can teach 'im some manners for the others, can't we, Capt'n?"

"Aye, teach 'im what twenty-five lashes can do; but that's the extent of it."

It took four seamen to pick up Mongo and hold his unconscious body against the mast, while two others tied his hands on high. They poured buckets of sea water on him until he regained consciousness.

Bojo laid aside the snake whip and picked up a cat-o-nine trimmed with lead pieces. He studied Mongo's naked muscular back for a moment and was impressed, even as he was about to disfigure it for life.

He raised the heavy cat-o-nine. "Try and eat my jugular, will ya?" The first blow brought welting stripes, the second, blood cuts, and by the sixteenth the entire back was raw and gushing with many deep furrows and recessions where the skin had been torn away. When the twenty-fifth blow landed, Mongo's body was convulsing; but throughout the ordeal, he was silent. Before they cut him loose, salt pickle was rubbed into his wounds to add to his pain and to prevent mortification. Then they threw him in the hold.

Blinking through bitter tears, Tilah blindly tried to follow after her husband. Two burly seamen blocked her way, grabbed her and dragged her away, screaming and fighting. The captain, busy with the helmsman, turned to the screams. He studied the youthful, well-developed body of the girl who was twisting and squirming between the two sailors who were about to whip her. "Leave her be. Take her below with the others," he shouted.

He watched them stow her away and noticed with approval that already the first mate was having the men swab the decks with buckets of sea water. The surgeon was making his way to the quarter-deck. The sea was getting rougher, and the brig was beginning to roll some; but he noted that the surgeon had no trouble in keeping his feet.

The captain started aft to talk with the helmsman, who was pointing to a black cloud fast approaching from the west.

"Captain," the doctor called. "May I see you a moment?"

"Yes?"

"What do the floggings really accomplish?"

"Just what do you suppose? What do you think we would have on our hands if we didn't show those heathen who their masters were? When we first get 'em aboard we kick hell out of 'em. Break 'em down. Put fear into 'em. Like taming wild animals. Only these animals can think, so they're dangerous. If you let them get a slight edge, you'll regret it. If we'd let that big Ashantee go unpunished, we'd a had a jolly time the whole passage, I guarantee. Look, Doctor, my patience is sorely pressed. I'm responsible for this ship and cargo to the company and no one else. I'll not have you questioning my authority every turn. I hope for your sake you understand me fully."

The wind was stronger now, and the captain was holding to the rail with both hands.

"Captain, I understand you fully," doctor Bass shouted into the wind. "I'll not press the subject. But I want you to understand, too, that I've taken an oath to treat men's ills and to save their lives whenever I can. I'll not go back on that oath."

The captain turned and went below. The surgeon walked to the port rail and studied the frothing sea. His mind and body recoiled, repulsed at cruelty so monstrous. He knew it must stop somehow. It must!

Chapter Four

Most of the crew had finished their tasks and had scrambled below. Those on watch were busy tying themselves to their stations with hemp. The second mate, Sarpo, was in harness at the wheel. Caution told the surgeon to go below, but his curiosity to know a tropical storm gripped him. Climbing to the quarterdeck, he found a dangling length of hemp and coiled it several times around his left hand.

"Doc," Sarpo said between glances at the big compass in the polished walnut binnacle before him. "I hope it isn't a lesson you're after. I'll be havin' me hands full for a bit."

"No, Sarpo. Just want to see for myself."

"Capt'n won't like it."

"Capt'n's below."

"Aye, I seen him go. Figured he would."

The full force of the squall hit then. A blast, as sudden and loud as a thunderbolt, struck the Zong and prostrated her nearly on her beam. The doctor was thrown down. He rolled leeward and into the quarterdeck's rail. When he got up, he saw Sarpo on one knee, hanging gamely to the wheel. The doctor attempted to help the mate.

"Okay, Doc!" Sarpo yelled. "Not hurt bad."

"Rest a minute!" the doctor shouted back. He took the wheel, only to find there was no power in the tiller. The ship was leaning so far before the blast that the tiller was half out of the water. A great tearing noise sounded over his head. He looked up to see the main sheet split neatly in two, then disintegrate into shreds from the bolt-ropes. The ship righted herself as the pressure was relieved.

Sarpo was on his feet trying to fix his broken harness. "Keep the lubberline on north, bearing sixty-five degrees east," he yelled through the driving rain. "I'll spell ya soon's I get hooked in again."

Doctor Bass did his best to keep the ship headed on course. While spending leisure hours with Sarpo and holding the wheel occasionally on the quiet voyage from Baltimore, he had never imagined what a tiller-in-storm was like. The pull of the wheel was abruptly strong, then easy. It seemed impossible to keep the lubberline corrected. The wind drove the rain almost horizontally over the water, stinging his face. When Sarpo was in position, Doctor Bass gladly surrendered the wheel.

"I'll find someone to relieve you so we can check that knee," the doctor said.

"Nay, Doc, let her be. The mate'll not approve. I've got to stay the watch, hurt or no."

The doctor made his way carefully down the companionway to the main deck. He was beginning to feel the effects from the ship's constant bucking. Voices crying in agony came to him through the wind, and for the first time he realized what it must be like for the slaves. As gusts of chilling winds blasted through his wet clothes, he worked his way along the storm line to the main hatchway. The air grating of the slaves' hatchway was covered with a heavy tarpaulin. Laboriously, he unlaced the canvas. On the ship's next dip into the sea a high wave swept over the deck and poured into the slaves' hold. Now, he saw the reason for the cover. Someone grabbed him savagely by the shoulder.

"You tryin' to sink this vessel, Mister?" Bojo snarled at him.

"I . . . I didn't realize. I was afraid they'd suffocate."

The mate ignored his explanation and replaced the lacings. Doctor Bass held tight to the storm line as the wind battered him and he fought the sickness and the sense of defeat that was slowly enveloping him.

Somehow he found his cabin. He fell into his bunk without bothering to undress. All through the night, as the storm pummeled the ship, he lay in feverish torment. Then, as darkness evolved into light, it became quiet; and the soft slap of the peaceful sea against the ship's hull and the lullaby of creaking timbers put him to sleep.

He awoke to loud shouting and the sound of shuffling overhead. He changed his wet clothes and hastened to the deck, urged on by the sound of a cat-o-nine cracking. The bright sun hurt his eyes, but he could see that the slaves had been brought up and were being fed from the kettles. Fifty percent were unable to stand. They sat or lay on the deck covered with their own filth, sick and weak, some near death from having been without ample air for so long a time. He counted over forty corpses.

A seaman was whipping a young boy who lay on the deck, while the captain and first mate stood close by. The surgeon's first thought was to help some of the others, but the boy took priority. He walked over to the captain.

"Mornin', Captain," he said nonchalantly. "Quite a

storm we had."

" 'Lo Sam. I heered you was galavantin' around in the middle of it."

Doctor Bass reddened. The tarpaulin blazed in his mind, and he realized the captain would think he had been interfering again. But the cries of the boy blotted out his self-concern. He cleared his throat.

"Why is the boy being whipped?"

"He won't eat. Most of them won't. But they'll learn from him."

"The heavy storm might have made them too sick to eat."

The captain did not reply. Doctor Bass caught the smell of rum and wondered if the captain had been too drunk to have known the storm's severity.

"Capt'n," said a seaman holding the boy. "He still won't eat."

"Bring 'im 'ere, then. By God, he'll eat if I handle 'im.

They dragged the young boy by his heels to the captain. He lay at the head man's feet, wild-eyed with fear.

"Gimme' a bowl of that pram," the captain barked. He took the bowl and offered it to the boy.

"Eat?" he asked in Ashantee.

The boy showed no sign of having heard.

The captain bent over and put it close to his face.

"Eat!" he demanded, and put the food to the boy's tightened lips. The boy turned away.

The captain angrily slammed the bowl down on the boy's head, and the white farina ran down the boy's chin and onto his chest. The captain pulled out a bolus knife from his belt; and, dropping to his knees, he held the boy's face against the deck. He tried to pry open the boy's mouth with the point of the blade. He managed to part the lips, cutting them in the process; but he was unable to get the blade between the teeth.

"A maul and chisel," he ordered, straightening up.

"For God's sake, captain! What will you prove!" demanded the doctor.

The captain did not reply but received the tools. While one sailor turned the boy over and held his legs, another took his arms and brought them up alongside his head and held them together. The captain sat down heavily on the boy's chest and, taking the chisel, put the edge between the boy's lips. Still, the boy did not open his mouth, nor did his face change. His big round eyes began blinking more quickly.

The doctor made a move to intervene, but two seamen grabbed his arms. The doctor turned to the sea; but from the corner of his eye he saw the hammer raised, heard the hard sound of cracking teeth as the chisel went in, and saw the hand spike prying the mouth open. The captain poured the farina down the boy's throat, causing him to gag.

"You'll eat tomorrow, I'll warrant," the captain said. He looked around at the rest. "Any others don't like our pram?' he shouted in native dialect.

When the surgeon was released, he moved among the slaves doing what he could for each and administering sulpher or spirits. It was not until he had treated half a dozen men that the shock waves within him began to subside.

When he came to Mongo, the big Ashantee was sitting with his eyes closed. Doctor Bass touched his arm. Instantly, the black man's eyes flashed opened. Mustering up a smile, the doctor rubbed his own arm and pointed to Mongo's back. Mongo looked away.

Doctor Bass examined him. The ugly lacerations were festering. He cleaned the wounds and sprinkled sulphur into them.

When he was done, Mongo looked at him and said something that Doctor Bass did not understand. But the fierceness had left his eyes. The doctor pointed to himself. "Bass," he said. Mongo looked at him curiously.

This time, when the slaves were ordered into the hold, they would not go until they were beaten with clubs and whips; even then many of them were thrown in. Mongo was one of the last, and Doctor Bass stood near him so that he was not beaten. The Ashantee did not resist. He stood tall and climbed down the three steps into the hold.

Bojo, red-faced and panting from the exertion with the slaves, approached the surgeon. "Looks like the big ox lost all his fight. You bother over 'em, Doc, like they're your own kin. Too much fussin', I say."

Angry and heartsick, the doctor glared at Bojo, and stomped away. He made his way aft to the captain's quarters and knocked at the door.

"Yeah?" a slurred voice answered.

The captain was sprawled out half naked in his bunk, sweating profusely and nursing a dram of rum. The cabin was hot, the stench sickening.

"Ah, Doctor, come in, come in, be comfortable. Would ya like a drink? The heat won't bother ya near as much. It'll be a scorcher today, I tell ya."

The doctor was amazed at the man's changing moods. Since he had a touchy request to make, the surgeon decided to accept. When the captain made no move to pour the drink, he helped himself from the bottle on the floor beside the bunk.

"Captain, how many slaves do you hope to land at your destination?" the surgeon asked, downing the rum slowly.

"Well, we shipped near five hundred. If I can land two-fifty, I've made money for the company. If you'd like to know how much . . . Well, figurin' four hundred a head as a good average . . . take away a slave for each crewman's share . . . it adds up to about seventy-five thousand dollars."

"You could actually lose half the lot and make that much profit?"

"You've got it right, laddie."

"That explains it then."

"Explains what?"

"The brutal treatment."

The captain stared at the ship's overhead beam. Finally, he said, " 'Bout two years ago, Doctor, I shipped a load of four hundred blacks out of Sierra Leone for a West Indies outfit. During that passage I lost all but a hundred, mind you. And do you know how I lost them? By starvation. The blasted fools went on a hunger strike. I personally lost fifteen thousand dollars. That's never goin' to happen to me again. I nip it in the bud with an example or two. You see, Doctor, as usual, your ignorance of this trade is gettin' in the way."

The surgeon held back a retort. He chose his words carefully. "I have a suggestion that could land you more healthy slaves at the end of your journey. I've not been in the hold as yet, but isn't it true that the women up forward breathe their air from the two hatchways aft that supply the men?"

"Aye," the captain said, yawning.

"Well, I've noticed we have lost more of the women from suffocation; and it seems a needless loss. If a hole were cut forward just big enough not to allow a slave to get through, the women would get more air."

"How would you keep the sea out in a squall?"

"Side boards and a tarp should suffice."

The captain closed his eyes.

The surgeon waited for a moment, then asked, "Well, what do you think?"

"I'll give it me best thought," said the captain. He rolled over with his face to the wall. The surgeon looked up at the cutlass hanging over the bunk, and then at the captain's bare back. All he would have to do would be to reach up, take the cutlass, and strike at the neck, and a mistake of nature would be eradicated. He hung suspended between two actions. Then he turned and stomped out.

Chapter Five

The Zong moved steadily northwestward, aided by westerly trade breezes and the south Equatorial current. But each day that she drew nearer the Equator the winds became weaker. By the end of the nineteenth day she was doing only four knots, though from deck to royal, from flying jib to ringtail, every stitch of canvas that would draw was packed and crowded on her. At the end of the twentieth day when she had not even traveled one nautical mile, the crew knew they had reached the low-pressure belt of equatorial calms where the great trade winds meet, called the Doldrums. As the brig rolled gently in the quiet sea, her great sails limp, uneasiness began to spread over the ship.

Day by day the hot, sultry air became more and more unbearable; and the men sweated and swore and fought and would have killed one another had it not been for the first mate. They feared him more than the captain, who was now constantly in his cabin, lost in a drunken stupor.

With little to do the men fell upon a new pastime. The square hole forward that the captain had permitted to be cut always seemed to have a black female head sticking out of it. Since a head blocking the hole meant less air for the others below, the surgeon asked the sailors to keep the heads below deck.

Unknown to Doctor Bass, however, the sailors complied by using the heads for target practice. When a marlinspike found its mark, a hit was scored; and they would roar and congratulate each other.

When several more such days passed, the water ration was cut to half a pint a man. The doctor spent most of his time above decks tending to the slaves, or to the increasing ailments of the crewmen. Occasionally, he visited with Sarpo when he had the watch at the helm. The second mate, flattered at being able to tutor a more educated man, showed the young doctor the finer points of navigation, demonstrated how to take sights for meridian altitude on the stroke of noon, and helped him figure the ship's position on the charts.

One evening the doctor and Sarpo were at the helm and were watching the sun dip down through dramatic cirrus clouds and slip slowly over the horizon. "How did you ever happen to sign on a slaver, Sarpo?" the surgeon asked, studying the striking scene.

"Sign? Humph! That's enough to make me poor dead father's corpse do a jig. I wouldn't have been caught dead volunteerin' to serve in this trade of the devil."

"You're the first seaman I've heard talk against this trade. How deep do your thoughts go on the subject?"

The mate spat to the side.

"Deep enough to know that the white man has started somethin' that in the years to come will prove his undoing. All for the lust of gold. But it's the God-awful mistreatin' that fills me with dread. This is my sixth voyage, and I keep tellin' myself that this is the last. But then I gits my pay, double at that; and the devil's got me once more. One more voyage, I keep saying; and I'll have me enough for a little cottage, maybe up high on a California bluff overlookin' the sea. But something always comes up to stop me."

"Why do you get double pay?"

"Well, not many know it so I'd appreciate your confidence . . ."

"You can trust me."

"Well, I don't have to tell you the captain loves his rum and his women. There's been times he gits on a jag and stays below for days. He gives me charge to navigate then."

The seaman spat again and looked around for eavesdroppers. "Frankly speaking, Doc, this is the worst I've seen 'im. He was always mean, but now he's sunk to a coward atop of it."

"Coward?"

"Aye. Did ya wonder why he never showed hisself even once during that squall that hit us, even after we lost our main sheet?"

"I did."

"I'm convinced he was skeered as a babe and a-suckin' on a bottle all through it, too. At first I was dumb but then I noticed . . . every voyage I ever served with him . . . come up a black Lucifer, and he'd be off like a cur with his tail under him. Oh, put a whip in his hands and see how brave he is with a helpless black. But the tragedy is that there's hundreds of others just as mean as him over these people . . . beatin' 'em up, tearin' off their limbs. I dunno, I guess it's lust for money does it."

It was getting dark. The ship's lanterns were lit fore

and aft. The heat hung over the ship like a giant leech, sucking at the lives of blacks and whites alike. Stumbling footsteps sounded below and proceeded to the quarterdeck. It was the captain.

"Aye, how goes it?" the captain asked when he discovered the two men at the helm.

"Not too well, Capt'n. There's narry a spiff," answered Sarpo.

"Still in the doldrums, are we?"

"Aye, sir."

"This is the fifteenth day."

"Two weeks, already? How could it be? You lie."

"Two weeks it is, Captain," the surgeon said.

"So be it then. Let the devil take it all. Ah, the heat, will it never let go? How are the niggers doin', Surgeon?"

"They're dying."

"What is the count now?"

"I believe three-eighty."

"Is that little bitch with the big Ashantee still in good shape?"

"I believe so," the surgeon answered.

"Have her brought to my cabin," the captain ordered Sarpo.

"Aye," Sarpo said. He hurried below.

Though the deck was dimly lit by the single lantern that hung from the mizzen mast shroud, the doctor could see the captain was unshaven. He stunk from rum.

"How you be, laddie?" the captain smiled, putting his hand on the doctor's shoulder.

"All right," the surgeon answered coolly.

"How do you like our doldrums?"

"I don't."

"Aye, neither does this man. Heat's enough to fry a man's brains." The captain drew closer, his breath foul. "There's been many a ship didn't make it through the doldrums, laddie," he whispered, hoarsely.

The surgeon tried to escape the foulness.

"Three weeks. That's all the time we got. If we don't git out by then, we'll never make it to port before the barrels go dry.

"But say, laddie, come join me below. We'll have some special entertainment that'll help us pass the evening. 'Tis the absolute best remedy to free your mind from thinkin' about this furnace we got ourselves stuck in. Are you game? Or should I say, are ya man enough?"

"No thanks," Doctor Bass said, trying to hide the disgust he felt, but not succeeding too well.

The captain didn't notice. "Suit yourself, lad." He turned and staggered to his quarters.

Chapter Six

When Captain Albright got to his cabin, he turned up the overhead lantern hanging from the deckhead and sat down heavily. He saw the girl. She was crouched near his seaman's trunk, her eyes wide in fear. He studied her, then went to her and lifted her up. She stood with head bowed, but he could see enough of her brooding face in the dim light to realize that she was far more exquisite than he had realized. He lifted her chin with a finger. Her face appeared lighter than the average Negro's, and her delicate features strongly suggested Indian influence. He kept her chin up, but she would not lift her eyes. She was smaller than most, and quite young. He spoke to her in Ashantee.

"What is your name?"

She did not answer.

He pinched her chin between his thumb and finger.

"I said what is your name?"

She stood silent, refusing to look at him. He had never had one like her. But her coolness annoyed him, dampening his excitement.

"I like you," he said tenderly. "If you would like me,

I would be very good to you. I would give you presents." He could have her with force easy enough, and sometimes he had found that starting by force didn't necessarily mean ending by force. But something about her made the idea of using force distasteful.

He went to his sea chest and lifted the heavy lid. Rummaging around in a lifetime's collection of trivia . . . voodoo heads, lucky pieces, some tools . . . he found a cheap pearl bracelet.

"To show you that I like you, I will give you this precious bracelet that will make all the other women envious of you." He held out the trinket. She did not respond, but just stood studying the open sea chest. Gently, he took her arm and slipped the bracelet on her left wrist.

"There, that is yours to keep," he said. "If you will not fight me, I will give you a necklace that matches the bracelet perfectly."

He reached over, picked up the bottle of rum, tilted her head back, and put it to her lips. She began to choke, and he took the bottle away. When she regained her breath, he made her drink again.

He set the bottle down and caressingly took her arms and put them around his neck. He stroked her, but he might as well have been stroking a dead woman. He studied her briefly, then made up his mind. He would put life into her in a way she wouldn't forget, by violence if necessary. But not tonight. He was heavy with rum and fatigue. He went to the door and yelled for Sarpo to come for her.

Tilah returned to her place in the hated slave hold. As soon as she arrived, hands moved silently over her body in the darkness to see if she had been hurt. She was asked many questions. What had she had to do? Did she have to make love to the *buckra*? Did she fight and try to claw out his eyes as Xata had done, or did she drink his rum and not fight as the tall Mau Mau who came back smiling and stinking and wearing a handsome bead necklace. Then the hands found the bracelet, and they sniffed at her. She felt them draw away, heard the name Mongo whispered many times. She was left alone then with her thoughts.

She thought of the *buckra*, and a chill ran through her. She couldn't understand how the big one had been able to do it. She had seen women become untrue many times, and she thought it had much to do with their men. But, of course, they couldn't all be like Mongo. Mongo . . . so wise, so manly! How happy she had been being his wife! He was respected by all. She was certain that the boys would grow up to be like him; Mongo had carefully taught them the ways of men. Somehow, she was sure they were safe. But would Mongo believe that she had not willingly been with the white man? "Oh, Mongo," she gasped half aloud, "don't let these wicked tongues poison your mind."

The chanting began again, the monotonous song of death. She despised it because she did not believe as the others that they were being herded to the white man's land as game to be cooked and served at his table. As she listened to the mournful crying of her people, a burden for them much stronger than her concern for herself or her love for Mongo filled her; as the long night gave way to a new day and the ship still lay quietly on a dead sea, she made her decision.

When the slaves were let up for the meal on a deck so hot it burned their feet, Tilah cast a quick look toward the captain's deck and hurried to her man. She was relieved to see that his eyes looked clear and did not show the sickness she noticed in more of the other men each day. She smiled when he looked at her and then tended to his back. He pulled away at her touch.

"It is better," he said.

She hesitated. "I should clean the flesh."

"It is better," he said more firmly. "Go eat." He turned away.

She moved to face him. "Mongo," she said tenderly. "Why do you speak so?" Then she saw that he was staring at her wrist. Her hand moved involuntarily to cover the bracelet. His eyes traveled up her body and then slammed into hers.

"The captain gave it to me last night," she said, "for nothing."

Mongo turned away and headed for the big kettle, the man chained to him moving as his shadow alongside.

"Mongo," Tilah called. "I said for *nothing*!" She started after him, but she stopped when she saw the figure on the high deck staring down at her. His eyes moved slowly up and down her body. For a while she did nothing. Then, conscious of the eyes of her people who were watching her closely and knowing that Mongo had turned and was watching her, too, she realized that there might never be a better opportunity. She looked up at the captain and smiled. At once, obscenities were hissed at her. The captain began to pace the deck shouting orders. Several men went below. Two others shouldered their way through the blacks and took her down to the captain's quarters. Just before she went down, she looked over her shoulder and saw Mongo looking out to sea. His face was ugly with emotion.

The two men led her to the cabin she had already visited. She stood by the table, while the men lounged in the doorway where there might be a small breeze, waiting for the captain. As before, the big chest stood in the corner with its lid open. Shouts sounded from above, and running steps pounded through the deck. One of the men climbed up the stairs and called down.

"It's that big nigger! He's gone wild! He's trying to get down here. Come on up! We better give 'em a hand."

The second seaman went up the stairs, and Tilah flew to the chest. In a frenzy, she scratched through the junk until she found it: a small flat file. Seizing it, she ran her fingers over its sharp roughness; and though she had never held one before, instantly reasoned its purpose. The noise overhead suddenly stopped. The captain's voice bellowed orders. Steps sounded on the stairs. Trembling in panic, she dipped her fingers in the tallow of the candle on the table and smeared the file. The steps stopped as the captain's voice called out a command. She smeared the last of the file, and put her head back. She might have tried another way, painful as it would have been; but there was no time to experiment. Steps sounded on the stairs again, heavy and deliberate. The file was in her mouth. Gently, she urged it down her throat. She gagged, withdrew it an inch. The steps were near. She could see boots. The file was half in. One final nudge. It slipped down her throat. Quickly, she turned to the chest and picked up a necklace.

"Ah, so we have found a necklace, have we," the captain said, smiling. He took the necklace from her hand and put it around her neck. He said softly, "That man of yours has an iron head. But don't fret, he'll be full of vigor, come morn." He kissed her, and his foul breath made her turn away. As he caressed her, she began to die inside.

"No hurt Mongo," was all she said before the horrible ordeal got under way.

When it was almost dark he let her go, sick and stinking of rum.

This time there were no questions. There were no hands to caress her caringly. Through the night she sat in the hated slumped position; but now sitting forward made the file stick her, and she would cry out. No one came to her. She could not sleep for the pain. To forget the pain she thought of her sons climbing through the giant mangrove trees that grew near the village. As the night wore on, as the death chant continued, her misery lingered; and when the slaves were called out in the morning, she barely managed to climb to the deck.

Mongo sat alone. His eyes were swollen and crusted. Blood matted his hair. His arms were chained behind him. Tilah sat beside him and waited for him to speak. The sun was a torment. She was very sick.

"Do you hurt much?" she asked.

No answer.

"Mongo, I was with the *buckra*. I was able to get a tool."

He ignored her.

"When I was with the *buckra*, I was able to take the tool and put it down my throat. It is here." She touched her abdomen. "It pains. I think it is cutting into me." Her voice broke. "Mongo, I fear. I didn't know what could be done. Forgive me. Perhaps I can bring it out in the hold by putting my head to the floor; but if not, the women must open me here with the long nails of their hands."

He turned and looked long into her eyes. "You did such a thing? Tilah, why?"

"For you and for them, Mongo. They die each day. They will listen to you. Show them what to do . . . the tool."

"My thoughts were evil, my Tilah. Forgive me."

"No, Mongo. You could not help what you thought," she gasped, paining again.

"I cannot allow this. I will speak to the friendly one with the medicine." He began to rise.

"No," Tilah pleaded, grabbing him. "Trust no one. This is the only way. You know this is true, please."

Mongo brooded. "I will kill the white devils. I will make them pay." He was quiet for a while, and then he wept softly. After a time he said, "Is there no other way, Tilah?"

"No, Mongo. I fought with my spirit at great length. My spirit told me that I could save our people from this cruelty. I love you Mongo, more than life; but I know that what I want is not so important now."

As the time came for their return to the hated hold, the whips cracked again. They tried to see each other as long as possible. She saw Mongo go down, and suddenly the pain was so severe she was aware of nothing but sitting on the deck and vomiting blood.

Chapter Seven

Three nights later a southeast breeze began to blow, and the ship sailed steadily once more. While the crewmen rejoiced at having left the doldrums, a young, pretty Negro woman died. The next morning they threw her torn body overboard, and the Captain was sure that she had been murdered because of him.

When Mongo was told that Tilah had died, he showed no outward emotion. He asked for the file; and then he told the people that if they wished to be free, they should do exactly as he directed. They could, of course, choose someone else to lead; but they would not.

First, they would try to cut four links a night, separating eight men. To avoid detection, the cut links were to be smeared with human waste and left unopened until he gave order. The chanting would continue at night to cover the noise.

When all this had been accomplished, and only then, they would cut the hatch lock and swarm from the hold like the locusts in the legend and devour everything in their path. And so, as the ship moved steadily northwestward, night after night the black people in her bowels sweated and strained as though possessed. When the file was dropped from exhaustion, another hand would snatch it up and grind away; and because the chains were of soft iron, six, eight, and even ten links were filed in a single night.

It was on the tenth night since the southeast trades had begun blowing that Sarpo stood at the rudder enjoying the cool winds on the back of his neck. As the Zong clipped along at ten knots, with spray flying, he imagined himself her master. He hadn't told the doctor that one very important reason he hadn't left the Zong was that under Captain Albright he could be a master without a master's worries.

Bojo, the first mate, was on the main deck talking with two sailors on watch. Another sailor lounged near the bow smoking a pipe, and Sarpo could just make out the man's form in the moonlight. He was rubbing his eyes, which had been bothering him lately, when he saw a figure leap across the deck. Then another. And another... until the deck was filled with shadows. He grabbed the ship's bell.

Bojo and the two guards fought well before they were killed. Others of the crew swarmed on deck with knives and cutlasses and attempted to hack their way through the rebels to the carronades. The captain appeared and fought his way along the rail to the swivel gun on the starboard side. When he reached it, he lit the ready fuse. A dozen black men screamed and fell as the big gun spewed death. The living froze and stared at the smoking monster.

Hesitating only an instant, Mongo screamed and grabbed the foremast shroud. With powerful hand-over-hand movements, he reached the captain, who was reloading. The captain looked up in time to swing the heavy ram rod. It struck Mongo in the forehead, but he didn't go down. He clutched the captain's throat with his left hand and grabbed the ram rod with his right. He shoved the captain back against the rail and had raised the rod as a spear to drive it through him when he was jumped by several sailors swinging marlin spikes and iron bars. He fought valiantly, but finally he went to his knees. They beat him more, till he rolled over on his back senseless. By now the sailors on the main deck were getting the best of the black men who, seeing Mongo go down, had lost heart. As the sailors overcame them, they threw them into the hold until only a band of twenty were holding out with their backs to the bow. When the captain saw that the slaves would jump overboard before they would be recaptured, he yelled, "Let them be, men." And they held to a stalemate through the night. In spite of his protests, Doctor Bass was only allowed to treat the crew.

In the morning the captain appeared topside and addressed the slaves in their tongue. "Lay down your weapons, and your lives will be spared," he shouted. "You do not have to die. You will not be harmed."

One of the natives, who had cutlass wounds on his arms and chest, said, "If we go there, we will die anyway." He pointed to the dark hold.

"You will not die," the captain answered. "If you do not cause trouble, you will live; and soon you will be on land again."

"Where are you taking us?" another black holding a fish iron demanded.

"To an island called Cuba. You will cut trees and work to make sugar, rum, and tobacco."

The natives discussed it. The captain waited. He hated losing twenty healthy stock.

The wounded man asked, "Will we be free men at this place?"

"You will not," the captain said loudly. "You know of warring by kings and the taking of slaves in your country. It is a thing you know well. If a man is lucky, he does not fall into slavery. You were not the lucky ones. But in this new place life will be much as it was in your country. Many of your people are already working there, and they are happy, for they are well cared for."

"Some of us believe you will sacrifice us there to your gods."

"This is not true," the captain said strongly, shaking his head.

The slaves converged together once more. Several minutes elapsed, but it was plain they disagreed.

The captain called for Mongo. They dragged him to the quarter-deck, chained hand and foot, and dropped him at the captain's feet.

"Tell your men to surrender," the captain ordered in Ashantee.

Mongo seemed not to hear.

"Your men cannot win now. If they jump into the sea, they will be destroyed. If they surrender, I guarantee no harm to them."

Mongo snorted. Water and blood ran down his chest making a pinkish foam. His Ashantee was labored.

"*Buckra* evil. No matter. Better that they die fighting as warriors than to go back into hell-hold like snakes and never see day again."

"That's rot! Of course they'll see day again."

"Many cannot. Eyes sick."

The realization was slow in coming. The captain had seen the inflamed bloodshot eyes of many of the slaves, but he had paid it little thought. He walked to the hold and looked down into the blackness. He had several slaves brought up and, keeping his distance, he looked into their eyes. All were bloodshot. Pus ran from most; three of the eight selected at random were totally blind. Shaken, he returned to Mongo. He noticed that the big man's eyes were clear.

"I know a way to help your people. Tell them to disarm, and I will have our medicine man tend to their eyes."

Mongo looked long at the captain. He remembered the surgeon. He thought about it, then made his decision. He tried to get up. Help was offered, but he shook it off; and, despite his chains, he managed to prop himself against the rail.

"Do not fight more," he commanded. Reluctantly, the slaves dropped their arms. Immediately, they were seized and taken aft where new shackles were attached to their ankles. The surgeon was called up from his quarters.

"We've a pestilence aboard, Doctor," the captain said when he arrived. "The slaves got it. Don't know about the crew."

Doctor Bass went to a young black who was not yet fettered and examined his eyes. The captain peered over the doctor's shoulder.

"Never seen the likes of it. What do you s'pose?"

Doctor Bass moved to another slave, the captain after him; and then he examined the crew. Daylight revealed what had been hidden by darkness. Many were infected.

"Do your eyes itch?" he asked a sailor who squinted noticeably.

"No," the man said quickly.

"Do you have any matter in them when you awake in the morning?"

"Aye, now that you mention it, they have been cloggin' a bit. The sun's been a bother lately, too."

The doctor turned away.

The captain grabbed his arm. "Look here, tell us . . ."

The surgeon pulled his arm away. "I will tell you, in private."

"No!" a voice demanded; and a skinny sailor, whose scarred and beaten face bore a cobra snake tattoo on his forehead, stepped forward.

"Beggin' your pardon, Capt'n," he said from the corner of his mouth, "but we in the crew thinks we've a right to 'ear it, too."

The surgeon looked from the man to the captain, then at the men. Silence reigned.

"What you have to say, say it here," commanded the captain.

"I am not positive," began the doctor. "I've never seen this disease before. But if it is what I've heard and read about it, it could be opthalmia, a severe and highly contagious eye disease that attacks and causes blindness in rapid order. Some call it 'red eye'."

The crew looked at one another.

"What hope is there, Doctor Bass?" asked a man the doctor had liked in the past for his mild nature.

"Hope?" the doctor asked. "Who's to say? There's always hope."

"What's the cure, man? That's what he means!" a gruffer voice demanded.

"The treatment is silver salts administered to the infected area, but there's none aboard."

Fear crept across the deck and clung to every man's soul. A slave moaned in the hold. The sea slapped and gurgled against the ship's sides.

"Some of you may not get it. Everyone should bathe with a sulphur solution that I will prepare. And, above all, everyone must keep clean."

"It's those niggers give it to us," the man with the tattoo cried. "We ought to throw 'em all overboard right now, and we'd have no pestilence!"

"That's enough of that talk now," the captain said. "What would you do with your comrades? Throw them over, too? Besides, are you forgettin' your wages are down there?" He pointed to the dark hold. "That's black gold down there, man, what's left of it. Now you men heave to. I smell a good breeze comin' up. Clear the deck for running. The doc'll get to each man in turn."

The men sulked as the captain ordered them about to take every advantage of the new wind. Some drew water from the sea and swabbed the decks. The captain put his hand on the doctor's shoulder.

"Laddie, our lives are in your hands."

"How soon will you bring up the slaves?" the doctor asked coolly. "I must treat them as soon as possible."

"Aye," the captain said, "We've got to find the file they used to cut those shackles."

At noon, as the Zong dipped and splashed through the whitecapped sea at 12 knots by the log line, the crew, having all been treated, armed themselves and were positioned around the slave pen. The slaves were herded to the deck in groups; and as the doctor walked among them segregating the blind, he bathed them with sulphur water.

It was only when the last group had been treated and searched that the file was found lodged under a head beam in the hold.

Forty-six blacks were totally blind.

"Line 'em up to the rail, men," the captain ordered. Men, women, and children were lined up single file facing the port rail. Some, too sick to stand, were carried.

"Break open the rail," the captain ordered; and the gangway rail was turned back on its hinges.

"Over the side with 'em, he said, and the first to go, a middle-aged man, stepped into his grave.

The surgeon was busy aft treating the sick. "My God," he cried when he saw the black head bobbing in the water. Running forward, he tried to grab the next slave in line, but was seized and held. And, as he watched helplessly, the forty-six were thrown to the sharks trailing the Zong.

As the last dreadful cries faded away, the captain turned to the shaken doctor. "Release him," he said to the sailors. "Just for the record," he said to the surgeon, "we're getting dangerously low on water. The doldrums hit us hard. Forty-six heads, that's twenty-three pints a day. We have to pay sixty dollars tax for each slave in Cuba, blind or no. And finally, maybe we can make a headway on the pestilence this way."

The doctor heard nothing he said. He had turned and was standing at the rail-gate, his fingers tightly clenched on its lock. As he stared aft at the ship's churning wake, the screams continued to reverberate in his mind.

Chapter Eight

Pushed by the steady tradewinds, the Zong made daily progress. Each new dawn found her two hundred miles closer to the isle of Cuba. The doctor ministered as best he could, sleeping only after the last man was cared for, some nights not sleeping at all. But his enemies—bad sanitation, bad nutrition, and no medicine — allowed the dreaded disease to attack and blind more of the crew each day. Sailors lay everywhere on tarpaulins and old sails spread across the main deck, and their moans mixed with the never-ceasing chant of the slaves.

It was late afternoon as the doctor moved from sailor to sailor giving each man a few drops of water from a supply that had dwindled to less than half a barrel. When he was finished, he went to the quarter deck where Sarpo, totally sightless, stood at the wheel, staring into the late afternoon sun. Sam Bass paused before stepping on deck and watched the courageous seaman guide the ship in frozen concentration, his strong hands moving the spoked wheel slightly one way, then the other.

"Sarpo, how goes it?" the doctor asked, trying to be cheerful.

"Fine, Doc, fine. A little parched, maybe; but we'll dance a Spanish jig in Havana yet." Doctor Bass took his canteen and held it against the mate's hand on the wheel.

"Drink this, friend," he said. Sarpo took a short pull on the cask. He gave it back to the doctor.

"That's all?" the doctor asked, surprised.

"Aye. Save it for the poor souls I hear on the deck."

The doctor took a long look westward, thankful that his eyes seemed as strong as ever.

"Sarpo, how is it you're able to stay on course?" he asked, looking at the lubberline. "Is your sight returning?"

"Nay, Doc. I sail by the sun in my face. The course we are on at present puts the sun in my face in the afternoon. It's crude sailing, I admit. Am I off far?"

"Only a hair to the north. Tell me, is there any way to estimate how many days we are from Cuba?"

"Hard tellin'. With the sheets unattended, I'll wager we've slowed up considerable. But the trades 'ave been steady enough. Say a week, maybe two on the outside. That is, if our course is true. We ought to have another reading. Don't think the captain will risk it, though. He ain't opened his door to me for the last week."

"I know. I tried again this morning. Every day it's the same. He doesn't acknowledge me either. Could be he's stricken, too."

A slight twinge of panic ran through Doctor Bass, but he fought it down. He scanned the horizon for a sign of land. He said an "Our Father", as he had found himself doing many times in the past few days; and he began to think of the Bible's story of how Christ fed the starving multitudes by turning a few loaves of bread and fish into many. The last of the ship's store had been used up yesterday. He would settle for just a little miracle, a thunder storm to fill the barrels with fresh water.

"Doc?" Sarpo said.

"Yes."

"If we make it through this... will I see again, ever?"

Doctor Bass looked at the long stringbean clouds that dissected the western sky. "From what little I know about this pestilence, probably not. But who's to say for sure? Do you believe?"

"Believe? Believe in what?"

"The Almighty."

"The Almighty!" Sarpo sneered. "There was a time, maybe, when I was younger. But now, I don't know. Oh, it ain't my eyes that cuts me."

"What then?"

"Well, I don't understand a God that would allow men like the captain to be the cause of so much suffering."

The doctor started to answer, but the cries of the sailors begging for food and water rose up once again from the deck below. He thought it over once more, then made his decision.

"Sarpo. If the big Ashantee can still see, I'm going to let him out to help us."

"The one called Mongo? The one led the revolt?"

"Yes."

"It's a risk. He could kill us all."

"Yes, he could. But I don't think he will. I sense something."

Sarpo scratched at his beard. "He's still a savage, and he's crazy with hate for us."

"I don't know. He is different than the others. I think I can reach him, teach him the lubberline. If the trades continue to hold steady, among the three of us, we could get the ship to land."

"The captain'd have us jailed soon as we contact any authorities ashore."

"Maybe. But there's no other way. I'll take responsibility. Secure the wheel and come with me."

The two men climbed down to the main deck, the doctor guiding Sarpo through the sailors strewn about the deck. When they reached the slaves' hatchway, the doctor took out a pistol he had found on a dead officer that morning and cocked it.

"All right, Sarpo, help me with the hatch. Put your hand here." The men heaved and the hatch came up with great difficulty, creaking on its heavy hinges. The doctor crouched and peered into the dungeon. The foul stench, as strong as the upheavals of a blast furnace, drove him back, choking.

"Sarpo," he said, through his gasps, "call down for Mongo. Tell him I want to see him, that he won't be hurt."

The mate leaned over and yelled down in Ashantee. One of the sailors lying near called out to the others, "Maties, they're letting the slaves free." He struggled to his feet but fell back, too weak to stand. The doctor had turned to look at the sailor; and when he looked again at Sarpo, who was still speaking in Ashantee, he saw a black arm reaching out of the hold for Sarpo's throat. Before the doctor could cock his pistol, the arm had pulled the blind man into the hold. Sarpo's screams mixed with those of the savages. A strong voice called out in a native tongue, then the cries from the hold ceased. Suddenly, Mongo appeared and, looking up, spoke in Ashantee to the doctor. When he finished, the doctor called down.

"Sarpo, are you all right?"

"Aye, they got me down, though, Doc."

"What did he say?"

"He says he'll come up if I stay down here."

"Hang on, Sarpo, and listen carefully to what I say. Tell him I agree."

Sarpo relayed the message. Mongo said something to the slaves and pulled himself up on deck with great difficulty because of the wrist irons that kept his arms together. He got up slowly. He tried to stand straight, but winced in pain from frozen back muscles. Even in his stooped position he towered over the doctor by at least a foot. The doctor put a hand on his shoulder and looked at his eyes. They were still clear.

"Mongo, I need your help. Men are dying. I trust you. Will you help? Tell him, Sarpo." Mongo turned a little to listen to the man shouting from below. When Sarpo was done, Mongo looked into the doctor's eyes for a long time. Then he looked at the cocked pistol.

Putting the pistol in his belt, Doctor Bass said, "Mongo, if you help me, I will remove the irons from your arms and your legs. You will not be harmed, you or any of your people. The crew is helpless. The man in the hold is the only one left who can sail the ship. The captain has locked himself in his cabin. He won't bother you. But you must let the man up so the three of us can sail the ship to land. There is no other way." As Sarpo repeated his words, Doctor Bass took out the irons key Sarpo had given him earlier. He opened the wrist irons on the Negro's raw and infected wrists. Mongo rubbed his arms, his eyes never leaving the doctor's. The doctor thought he saw a flicker of gratitude. He knelt behind Mongo and opened the leg irons. With his left arm loose and touching the butt of his pistol, he faced the giant native.

Sarpo was handed up at Mongo's command. His face and neck were horribly clawed.

"You should have told me you were this hurt," Dr. Bass said to the mate. He dressed the wounds.

"I thought ole' Sarpo had seen his last, I'll tell you. But what do you propose to do with the big one?" Sarpo asked.

"Come, I'll show you," the doctor said; and he led Mongo and Sarpo to the bridge.

Sarpo took the wheel and corrected the course as specified by the doctor.

"Now explain to him what you're doing, mate," the doctor said. As Sarpo explained the workings of the ship in Ashantee, and then in English, so the doctor could point out various gear, Mongo listened attentively. When they finished explaining the lubberline, Mongo was given the wheel and, in short time, was holding the ship on a true course.

Mongo stood at the wheel for the next several hours and thought everything over carefully. Seizing the ship just now could be unwise. He had seen the empty ration barrels and the almost-depleted water cask, and he knew the only hope for any of them was to get to land soon. Only the whites had the knowledge to do it.

Though the southwesterly trades miraculously continued to blow gently but steadily, so that the sails needed no attention, five days later found the water supply depleted, with still no sight of land. Doctor Bass speculated that they might have missed Cuba completely. Then a realization hit him. The bright sun was beginning to hurt his eyes.

Two more days elapsed. The captain never appeared. Doctor Bass was no longer able to make the rounds. Sarpo was too weak to stand. Only a giant dark-skinned man from a dark land still held his feet, guiding the vessel that had been his torment ever westward. Doctor Bass was dimly aware that Mongo had let his people out of the hold, but he neither objected nor was afraid. He heard no struggles or cries. He lost his senses then.

A long dream later he felt wonderful cool water on his lips, and he looked up into the eyes of an olive-skinned man dressed in a blue uniform.

Chapter Nine

"Ah, you taste the water, si, Señor? Drink your fill. Later there will be food brought aboard for all."

"Who are you?" Doctor Bass asked weakly.

"My name is Juan Colerto. I own sugar fields near here. My man saw you run aground. You are the doctor, si?"

"Yes."

Doctor Bass wanted to ask other questions, but he was too weak. There were men everywhere armed with long broad knives and muskets, and they were herding the slaves aft of the mizzen mast.

"Don't worry, we have things in control now. Your captain tell us everything." Colerto's face grew hard. "Since I am the District Magistrate, I must take you into custody."

They took Doctor Bass, Sarpo, the slaves, and the nine crewmen still alive and herded them into wagons. Guarded by heavily armed gauchos, they rode forty miles through heat and dust to Havana. There they were segregated: the whites sent to the garrison hospital, the blacks to big open pens, called barraccoons.

After two weeks, Doctor Bass was brought to hearing before the Captain General of Cuba. He had regained most of his strength, but his left eye was sightless. Only three members of the crew were fit to testify. Blind, helpless, fearful, they were easily intimidated; and they collaborated with the captain's version of the happenings aboard the Zong.

The captain looked well. His eyes were healthy. He had put on weight from the rich Spanish food and looked very authorative in his naval blues. His testimony was given in a quiet, matter-of-fact tone, without emotion, and was so convincing that even Doctor Bass doubted momentarily if he had acted wisely.

He thought of Mongo and knew the African would help him if he could. He asked to have the slave testify, but his request was unheard of and denied. He was ordered to appear at a hearing in Baltimore at the request of the company owning the Zong. Its owners were upset with their losses and needed a scapegoat.

Of the nearly five hundred slaves that shipped from Africa aboard the Zong, only one hundred were fit for sale at public auction in Havana. The remaining seventy, useless to the company because of their affliction and costly to the government because of their care, were taken out in tens during the following six weeks and quietly killed. The men who performed this task were private citizens and were paid five dollars a head.

The healthy sold at the average price of twenty-five doubloons for male adults ($400) and eighteen for females ($300). The bidding on Mongo finally stopped at thirty-seven doubloons after much heated shouting and oaths. A slave trader who carried black cargo from Cuba to New Orleans regularly bid the highest, sure that he would still make a large profit. His name was Harley Greene.

Like many of his compatriots, Harley Greene felt that dealing in the slave trade was a perfectly respectable profession. In nine years he had carried fifteen hundred blacks into bondage to the southern states. He saw Mongo as a magnificent animal capable of hefting big timber, or pulling a plow for long hours under a blazing sun, or prolonged stud service. He bought only two other males, having spent more than he had planned on his prize.

His vessel was a twenty-two foot schooner, his crew, a Creek Indian for whom he had traded two horses in Savannah. The Creek was trustworthy and had a special way with the blacks.

When Mongo climbed aboard the schooner, he was not the specimen that had boarded the Zong three months earlier. His dissipated body bore tales of cruelty. Long, half-healed cat-o-nine stripes covered his back, and his wrist and ankles were still festering. A fresh scar dissected his broad forehead from nose to hairline. But still, there was a swagger to his step that invited caution. He was directed forward and chained by the feet to the foremast by the Creek, who tried to be careful with Mongo's ankles.

Mongo sweated in the sun all afternoon as the last provisions were being stored aboard. Sightseers on the docks stared at him as though he were some rare animal.

And then he saw him. He was walking along the dock and studying each schooner, stopping occasionally to ask a question of a crewman. He looked haggard and unlike Mongo remembered him. But as he drew closer, Mongo was sure—it was Doctor Bass.

Their eyes met and the doctor beamed. He ran to the schooner's side.

"Mongo. Thank God. How are you?"

Mongo understood very little. He smiled a little. The doctor spied a water bucket used by the dock hands and handed Mongo a ladle of water. The Creek Indian appeared topside. "No mess with slave. Master not like."

Doctor Bass straightened. "I know him. We were on the Zong together. I would speak with him for a moment. Do you speak Ashantee?"

The Indian looked around. Harley Greene had left for a forgotten provision and was due any moment.

"Speak, I help." said the Indian.

"Mongo, I was at the auction," Doctor Bass began. "I tried to borrow the money to buy you, but because of what happened, they would not give me credit . . . loan me money."

The Creek interpreted; and Mongo listened, studying the doctor intently.

"I'm sorry for what's happened. It's wrong. You are being sent to America to pick cotton and do other work. But I intend to resist this monstrous trafficking in human beings. I plan to stay in the South and convince the big landowners that one man owning another is.wrong. They will have to kill me to stop me from speaking!"

Mongo smiled a little at that. He remembered the doctor's stubborness with the captain aboard the Zong. He had heard of the trouble the doctor was having with the ship's owners. "What will they do to you?" he asked in Ashantee.

"They will have another hearing before a magistrate . . . a big chief. I'm not concerned. I have many friends. Some are lawyers and will advise me well.

"But . . . there's a thing I must say to you, and I thank God that he answered my prayer and brought us together." He paused to wipe the perspiration from his forehead and to gather strength. "I want to thank you for trusting me on the ship . . . even though . . . " he was having a hard time speaking. "Even though it kept you in bondage." He took a deep breath. "Not all whites are cruel. There are many who are kind. Don't let hatred rule your heart."

When Mongo heard the Creek interpret the last sentence he turned quickly away and stared out to sea. He did not look again at the doctor.

"But . . . the main thing I'm trying to say is, thank you for not taking our lives when you had the chance." Tears were brimming the doctor's eyes. He started to say more, but couldn't. He turned and disappeared in the crowd.

Long after the schooner had gotten under way, Mongo sat motionless staring out to sea. When the sun went down, he dozed and dreamed of a far-off land that burned with colors and of a woman who walked with him through the land and touched him softly. He awoke to find the Creek gently rubbing ointment on his ankles.

It was morning. The Creek smiled at him and held out a water cask. Mongo grunted, sat up, and drank his fill.

"Big man need big drink," the Creek smiled.

"You want savvy *buckra* talk?" asked the Creek, pointing to his lips. "Master say, I teach." And so he did. Because of blockade patrols, their voyage in the Gulf was delayed a total of eleven days, and they had a lot of spare time. Mongo knew "buckra" talk could be helpful in any escape attempt, so he cooperated. His keen mind grasped the words quickly, and soon he was putting short sentences together.

But Mongo learned more than English. He studied every move made in sailing the schooner. He noticed the heading was always northwest. He noted how the tiller, boom, and sheets were handled; and he kept track of the number of days. This information was stored away with all the things he had learned aboard the Zong.

His hate had not diminished. Though he did not intend self-torture, he thought of the beatings, the death chants, and Tilah almost constantly. One day he was sitting in the bow and looking out to sea when he realized that he was enjoying thinking of how he would avenge Tilah's death. This bothered him in the way that thinking about Doctor Bass had. Though thinking of Bass mellowed him, he became confused at the contradiction that this white man had not been cruel to him and his people. It was easier to hate. Hate gave him strength. It made him patient, ever waiting, watching for the opportunity to get free and taste revenge!

Chapter Ten

Although slave trading had been declared illegal by the 1897 Congress, the New Orleans docks swarmed with sweating blacks loading rum, tobacco, cloth, and slaves aboard the Guineamen bound for Africa.

Harley Greene chose not to pay under the table to the customs men and landed at a special cove he knew five miles below the main docks.

The slaves were hustled out quickly and herded up a steep bank. A small cabin lay well inside a stand of timber, and there the Creek was left to guard the slaves while Harley Greene went into New Orleans to "learn the market."

He returned that evening with a team of mules and a flatbed wagon. The five spent the night together, the slaves with their necks inside big rings that had been bolted into the heavy oak planking on the floor.

The next morning the Creek cooked up eggs, yams, and bacon; and when they had finished, Harley Greene dipped his fingers into the bacon drippings and smeared it around the slaves' mouths and over their bodies.

"Now youns' really look well fed," he said, wiping his fingers off in Mongo's hair.

They reached the trade yards around noon in plenty of time before closing. Harley was unhurried as he talked to the head auctioneer.

"I got three prime blacks in the wagon. Won't take less than fifteen hundred for the two younguns'. The big one's got to go for least twenty-five hundred."

"Twenty-five hundred!"

"You heard right!"

"What's his points?" the auctioneer asked, pencil in hand.

"Big, strong, fine, fine lines. Speaks English. 'Telligent, willing."

"Marks?"

"Oh, yeah, a few."

"Few, huh? Skills?"

"Heard tell he sailed a ship to Cuba when the crew took sick."

"O.K., bring 'em in," the auctioneer said, making a few final notes. He put the notebook into his back pocket and climbed up on a wooden platform, picking up a bullhorn on the way.

" 'Tention, gents," he yelled down in a twangy voice. "This is block seven comin' up. The right pen holds a young wench, three young bucks. Look 'em over. Look alive! Bidding starts in five!"

Mongo stood apart from the others in the pen. He stood tall, defiant, staring down the men in broad-brimmed hats who were gathering around him. Someone pulled down the shirt Harley Greene had made him put on to cover the scars, and the "ahs" went up from all around. He had gained back his weight; and though his muscles had not been worked in awhile, they were still harder than any slave seen at auction that day. Someone found a measure and announced his height at six feet, four and one-half inches. Chest, fifty-two inches; arms, seventeen inches; thigh, thirty inches.

The crowd grew larger. Hands probed into his mouth and ears and into the still tender scars on his back. His anger swelled with his humiliation. He was near the explosion point when the auction began.

A girl about fourteen was the first to go on the block. She wore a burlap bag that had holes cut out for her head and arms. Tears streamed off her cheeks, and Mongo's insides twisted. She resembled Tilah.

"What am ah offered for this portly, strong, young wench. She's never been 'bused," the auctioneer chanted. "What ah hear? What ah hear?"

"Five hundred," someone shouted.

"Ah hear five. Ah hear five. Do ah hear more? Do ah hear six?"

The Creek moved alongside Mongo and whispered, "Soon we part. Don't make fuss. You be fine."

Mongo studied the Creek and saw something he had seen before in someone's eyes . . . aboard the Zong. Something stirred within him. "Woman young," he said nodding to the girl.

"She husband sold morning. She never see him 'gain, likely," answered the Indian.

Mongo snorted and looked away. The fire was rekindled. The girl sold for five hundred and seventy-five. After much haggling, Harley's two young bucks brought twelve-fifty apiece. Mongo was then pushed up on the block.

He stood in the hot sun and sweated, and the sweat highlighted his sculptured chest and arms. The auctioneer was not too anxious for his scarred back to show.

"Gents, ah'm told this 'ere nigger ain't no ordinary nigger. He was a leader of the Ashantee strain, and anyone knows African stock knows Ashantees are sturdy workers and loyal to their masters. Ah'm also told this fine specimen practically sailed a slayer singlehanded when the crew come down with sickness. Now, what am ah bid for this magnificent specimen?"

"One thousand."

"Ah have a bid of one thousand dollars. Do ah hear twelve? Do ah hear twelve?"

"Thirteen."

"Ah have a bid of one thousand, three hundred dollars. Do ah hear more? Some lucky owner will get a fine stable from this prime stud. Do ah hear one thousand five hundred?"

"Fifteen hundred," said a new bidder in the rear.

Several turned toward the quiet voice. Daniel P. Ellem stood tall and well dressed, his narrow piercing eyes studying Mongo.

"Ah hear fifteen, do ah hear more?"

"Sixteen hundred," bid a young minister.

The bidding kept increasing until twenty-six hundred, and Ellem and the minister were alone. Ellem backed the minister down at twenty-eight, threw the cash down, and put a rope lasso over Mongo's head. The crowd watched as he half dragged Mongo off the platform to where his imported buggy was waiting and tied Mongo hand and foot in the back of it.

The big chestnut sorrel hitched to the buggy was Ellem's most prized property. Most horses trotted to keep up with her walk. She loved to run. Ellem gave her a loose rein and she started off on a trot which she continued the entire seventeen miles to the plantation. The last three miles he made Mongo run along behind the buggy.

When they reached the plantation, Ellem climbed down and untied Mongo, who fell to his knees.

"Git up, Nigger, no time to lolligag."

The house servants appeared, wide-eyed at the sight of Mongo. Some of the men, too old and feeble to work in the fields now, could vividly recall when Ellem had first brought them from the market and the steps taken to break them down.

They stood now, a dozen or so men bare to the waist in rough sewn britches, the women in simple gingham gowns. All were apprehensive of Ellem's next action. The conch shell sounded; and, shortly, Solomon, the overseer, appeared carrying a whip of plaited cowhide. He examined Mongo closely.

"Bin touched up some, ah reckon," he said, referring to Mongo's back.

" 'Bout half broken, ah judge," said Ellem. "Take a little."

"Make a fine stud, be good fer them fidgety wenches."

"Reckon," Ellem said half to himself. He took Solomon's whip.

"What's your name, Nigger?" he asked Mongo, who had gotten up and was breathing somewhat easier. Mongo played dumb, but Ellem wasn't fooled. He raised the whip and struck Mongo in the temple with the heavy handle. Mongo staggered back against the buggy and hung on to one of the wheels as the world went wild. Ellem rapped the fingers around the metal rimmed wheel with the handle, and Mongo lost his grip and started to fall. Two slaves grabbed him and propped him up against the buggy. Ellem stood very close to him.

"Now, what is your name?" he asked, very deliberately. Mongo lunged weakly at Ellem, but Solomon and two slaves grabbed him.

"Take him to the block," ordered Ellem, angered. They half carried Mongo to a wooden structure in the rear of the big house. His neck and wrists were put into a rack, and he was forced to stand bent over from the waist. Within minutes he could feel the strain on the back of his legs. He was left alone to think things over, and phase two of Ellem's "nigger bustin' " plan went into effect. An hour later demons were jabbing fire lances into his legs and his back. When he bent his legs to relieve the stress, the board dug into his throat. He ached for water. Several slaves came to gape at him, but they were forbidden to aid him.

It was almost midnight when Ellem came out with his two house boys. He had had a good dinner and half a dozen brandies and was in the mood for a black wench. He put his lantern against Mongo's cheek.

"What is your name, Nigger?" he asked.

Mongo was in a daze. Painfully, he was aware of the lantern burning him. He could just make out Ellem's sneering face beyond the blinding light.

"Mongo," he grunted hoarsely.

"Mongo? Well, well ah swore. And what do that stan' fer, that name, Mongo?"

Mongo tried to make his mind focus. White man's words came slowly to him.

"Mean king."

"King? Well, ah'll be. Ah got me a king," he said. chuckling drunkenly. But he stopped. A point had to be made. "You *was* king, savvy? Ah mean, when ah bought you, ah became your king. Ah'm king of all this. But to you ah'm *Master*! You is mine to do what ah want to do with, savvy? Ah can kill you right now, iffen ah take a mind. But ah won't kill you iffen you be a good nigger. You hop to it when ah calls you, savvy?"

Mongo was vaguely aware of Ellem's message. He wanted freedom more than anything.

"Yes, Master," he said, half-heartedly.

"Ah didn't hear that. Let me hear you say it once more. Say it, 'cause ah don't ever want you to forget it. Ah am your master. You am mah nigger. Right?"

Mongo ground his teeth. "Yes, Master," he said louder.

"That's a good nigger. Now you can be let out. But start kickin' up a fuss, and back here you come. Savvy?"

Mongo nodded. They had to carry him to the first cabin in line where he spent the night under the eye of Big Willie, the biggest and meanest lead row man on the place.

The slaves were called to work before daylight. Solomon went from cabin to cabin, rapping on the outside with his stick. Mongo, stiff and sore, ate the hominy grits and pork belly Will gave him. A solitary candle lighted the hovel, revealing the barest essentials: a clay pot or two, corn husk filled bags on wood platforms for sleeping, a small plank table high enough off the dirt floor to squat under.

After awhile they were ordered outside where they stood in line for crude hoes and rakes. Many of the women were pregnant. The youngest, an eight year old mulatto boy, stood shivering in a potato sack shirt that barely covered his bottom.

The line moved out and started down a hill to the

corn fields in the bottom. Willie started a chant the others picked up immediately:

Saturday night, and here ah am.
Young gals on my mind.
Workin' all day in the hot sun.
Young gals on my mind.
Mastah goin' to town, goin' to town,
Mary, does you love me now?

When the long line arrived at the river bottom, it was light enough to work. Immediately, they separated into groups of ten, each group bossed by its own "lead row nigger". Willie kept Mongo at his side and demonstrated how to scrape the weeds out from around the young stalks and heap the dirt up into little mounds.

Mongo caught on immediately and, exhilarated by the feeling of working muscles and crisp air, took to the work. By midmorning he was a full row ahead of Willie.

Solomon rode back and forth on an Albino filly and occasionally cracked his whip over a bent back. He noticed Mongo was ahead and riding up, said, "That big buck makin' you look sick, Big Wil. He keep it up an' ah got me a new lead row nigger, haw!"

"Yes, Boss," Wil agreed. Though he was only a notch above an ordinary field hand, he had authority. He wasn't about to lose it.

Mongo worked steadily, not even aware that he was in a contest, using his body naturally, gracefully with rhythm, not jerkily like some. When Solomon was out of range, Wil embarked on psychological warfare.

"Hey, boy," he began. "Ah knows you new, so's you don't know 'bout our ways. Iffen one nigger tries to outwork another nigger, then that's poison 'round here. Makes a heap of troublement."

Mongo paused, wiping his brow.

"One time a big buck named Luke come to the master in a trade. Most glad to hav'im 'cause he come on Saturday with a fiddle. Every Saturday night us has a frolic down in the gulley, an' he fair make the fiddle talk that night. The gals all cakewalkin' for 'im. Come Monday the troublement starts. All the men in the woods cuttin' fence rail. This big buck cut over a hundred foot of rail in the same day." Willie paused to think. Mongo, concentrating on Willie's story, rested on the hoe. Willie continued, making up ground.

"The Master sees this and don't like it 'cause he thinks we is not workin'. Next day he's out there hisself with a whup, an' man, did us niggers work! Howsomever, come night that big buck met with the Hoodoo men. They toted him off to the woods and hung 'im upside down by the heels till daylight. Then somebody went out and cut him down. Next day he ain't so bright-eyed and bushy-tailed. Ever time he falls behind he cotch the whup." Willie squealed with glee as he remembered.

Mongo didn't understand every word, but he got the idea. Solomon was coming their way. He started hoeing again and thought about Big Wil. When the time came to escape, he would have to contend with him first. He wondered if the Hoodoo men were real. He decided not to antagonize Wil for the present, and soon the lead row man was substantially ahead of him.

The afternoon dragged heavy and hot. As the sun moved higher, the heat from its mass poured down over the wooded crests, down the rocky slopes, and into the bottom lands, scorching everything. Even the little crawling things that lived by the creek burrowed into the cracks of its dried-up bed to escape.

A red-shouldered hawk, gliding high in the sky, scanned the creek bed with telescopic vision. It was too hot to sing, too hot to talk. The slaves sweated and cursed the dust and their parched throats and worked only out of fear of Solomon and his whip. Some overseers let a dropout have a drink and ten minutes in the shade, but not Solomon. A dropout was whipped into line or left lying. Late in the afternoon two young bucks and a pregnant woman in her thirties were whipped, and only the bucks made it back in line. When the conch horn sounded, Big Wil and Mongo were designated to carry the woman back. She moaned and carried on in spite of Mongo's attempts to comfort her.

They laid her on the husk mattress in the cabin; and her husband, a frail, wiry man who was only twenty-eight but looked twice the age because of years of heavy work, kneeled down beside her and swabbed her face. As Wil eyed the woman's fourteen year old daughter, Mongo stared at the scene of tenderness on the floor and screamed inwardly at another outrage committed against a helpless people.

They went back to the cabin and ate pone and hog belly in silence. It was Saturday night. Instead of getting ready for sleep, Wil put on a denim shirt and combed the grass out of his hair. He threw Mongo a shirt and bid him do the same, for they were headed to the frolic.

Most of the dancers were young, and they shuffled to clapping hands and the rasping squeals of an old fiddle missing two strings. Some of the bucks did a curious step called the jig, a high stepping motion at times, or a rapid flutter step. At times, the dance evolved into a reel or to the "pigeon wing", as couples manipulated together. Mongo was bewildered. It had been many moons since he had seen black people demonstrate such joy.

He and Wil sat down by one of the fires, and Mongo eyed the sweet potatoes roasting on sticks in the coals. Several young girls were doing a curious thing with pots that rattled and exploded; and when he was offered the white puffed balls, he was amazed that this delicious food had come from the stalks he had worked so hard cultivating that day.

The dancing sounds of the violin and the obvious joy spoke to Mongo as surely as any drum ever had. Everyone was either clapping or singing, and it wasn't long before he found himself nodding to the rhythm. Wil handed him a jug; but as soon as he smelled it, he made a disgusted motion and handed it back.

"What's matter, boy? You too trembly for corn?" Wil taunted. The men who had seen the gesture waited for his answer. Mongo knew he was being tested. Just as the dance ended and it was quiet for a moment, Mongo looked deliberately at each of the men and said, "In our land, brother sell sister, father sell son to war-man for rum."

They knew too well what he was saying, and some turned away as memories blazed back. Others smirked, and he was left alone to watch lithe females taunt those who watched their gyrations. Old passions that evolved into heart-severing memories of Tilah flooded him as he watched couples skip off into the bush for self-gratification and, consequently, to help Ellem realize his breeding goals. It was then he realized that the two young bucks who had been sitting across from him, the same two who had been beaten in the fields that day, were gone.

His attention returned to the dancers, especially to

one who had been eyeing him. After awhile, he got up slowly, walked over to her, and, taking her hand, led her into the darkness.

The frolic ended a short time before dawn. Mongo helped Willie climb the hill to their cabin, and, with the other happy, weary, half-drunk members of their displaced nation, they fell into the husk mattresses and slept soundly.

He was awakened by bright sunlight coming through the door of the cabin. Wil was snoring loudly. Mongo stood up and stretched his muscles, now stiff from the field work, and walked quietly to the door. The long row of cabins dipped down into the valley and continued up the hill on the other side. Straight ahead was the cornfield, on the hill to the left stood the big house, and to his rear was the woods. His thoughts began to quicken as he imagined himself running through the woods, staying in the densest foliage to slow down pursuers.

The conch horn sounded, bringing him rudely back to his senses. Solomon came into view from near the big house and headed down the hill toward him. He withdrew into the cabin, thankful he hadn't been hasty.

The plantation suddenly became a bedlam of activity. Curses, moans, and loud talking erupted as hangovers became real and last night's activity had to be explained to jealous mates. After much threatening by Solomon, the black society was finally assembled and marched up the hill to the yard of the big house to Sunday morning "church" service.

Martha, Ellem's wife, stood on the gallery of the big house and watched as the slaves assembled before her on the lawn. She wore a filmy blue chiffon dress trimmed with pink bows. Mongo and Willie sat up front and watched the breeze play with her dress, first revealing her slender ankles, then pressing the thin material against her body, revealing her ample figure.

Mongo watched her long yellow hair caress her cheek, then fly off to catch the sun's rays. He saw the flawless flower-like whiteness of her skin and the long slender hands that caressed the black book; and he became enraptured by the first white woman whom he had ever seen up close.

"Ah would pleasure to read to you all from the Gospel of John this mornin'," she smiled down at them. "But first, may we all bow our heads for a word of prayer?"

Dan Ellem didn't like it much, but he allowed Martha to read to the slaves from her Bible every Sunday. Encouraged by an occasional convert, she presented the gospel faithfully.

Now she bowed her head; and with eyes closed, she prayed for wisdom to teach her flock, for an end to suffering, and for the flock to love one another. Some of the flock bowed their heads, but a lot of the men kept their eyes on that dress and the things the wind did with it. Mongo noticed everything. His eyes traveled up to the delicate face, and he saw the look of rapture and peace. When she opened her eyes and looked straight at him, he suddenly thought of Doctor Bass. He began to listen to her words.

"We've come now to a very wonderful chapter in John. Remember, last worship time ah told you all we were goin' to learn about how a religious leader of the Jews named Nicodemus met Jesus and what Jesus said to him? Does anybody recall the story? Bess? Ruth? Benjamin?" Martha had given Biblical names to each newborn child and to each new convert upon being baptized. A white-haired slave in the rear slowly got to his feet.

"Miss Martha, ah disremember's 'xactly, but ah kin recollect most of it."

Martha was pleased.

"Well, tell us the story iffen you 'members it," she beamed. She couldn't remember his name, but she knew he was a horse trainer acquired in a big trading swap Ellem had made before Christmas. The man held his battered straw hat in both hands and looked around wide-eyed, pleased to be the center of attention.

"In the days of the disciples there was a small colored man name Niggerdemos that was a Republican and run a eating-house in Jeruslem. He done his own cooking and serving at the tables. He heard the tramp, tramp, tramp of the multitude a-coming; and he asked: 'What that going on outside?' They told him the disciples done borrowed a colt and was having a parade over the city. Niggerdemos thought the good Lord would cure him of the lumbago in his back. Hearing folks a-shouting, he throwed down his dishrag, jerked off his apron, and run for to see all that was goin' on; but having short legs he couldn't see nothing. A big sycamore tree stood in the line of the parade; so Niggerdemos climbed up it, going high enough for to see all. The Savior tell him: "Come down', we goin' to eat at your house, Niggerdemos.' Niggerdemos come down so fast, when he hear that, he scrape the bark off the tree in many places. Niggerdemos was sure cured of the lumbago, but sycamores been blistered ever since. Next time you pass a sycamore tree, look how it is blistered!"

The congregation's reaction was instantaneous. Laughter, guffaws, and "amens" came all at the same time. Martha was speechless. Just as she was about to correct the story, Dan Ellem strode menacingly into the center of the group. There was immediate silence.

"Mat and Luce run off last night," he said to no one in particular, pacing to and fro. "Jes, saddle a horse and git over to Dalyrimple's. Tell 'im to bring nigger hounds, iffen he's got any worth runnin'.

Jes, a house servant, sprang to his feet and ran to the barn.

"Where's Tom?" Ellem asked, looking around. Tom, the stable boy, stood up.

"Here ah is, Master."

"Ride down the line to each plantation and spread the word to meet here in two hours; and tell 'em all to bring hounds. Git!" The slave was off and running. Dan turned and seemed to notice Martha for the first time. He looked at the open Bible in her hands.

"Lot of good your preachin' does. Damn waste of time, ah say. Well, ah'll guarantee ya one thing, Miss Holiness. This time when ah catch them runners, nothin' you say or do is goin' to help em."

He stalked off with Solomon at his heels. Martha looked down at her flock and said nothing, just kept looking at them with that look on her face. They all knew what it meant. If caught, "second timers" seldom were allowed to live.

They were dismissed then and silently returned to their hovels, some to speculate, some to mourn death before it had come, some to pray. Willie and Mongo sat down in the sun and leaned their backs against their cabin.

"Them two got beat in the field 'tother day?" Mongo asked.

"Yep."

"What he goin' do?"

"Kill 'em likely," Willie answered, trying to get comfortable for a snooze. Mongo thought about it.

"He cotch?"

"Most likely. He don't give up."

"How he cotch?"

"Nigger hounds. They come from Cuba. You was there. See any?"

"No. They fast?"

"Like hell. Bring a man down, chew 'im up 'fore you kin bat an eye. Smell you out of a river bottom or out of a tree. Same thing."

"You ever run?"

"Never yet. Almost did. Got caught with the master's t'baccer pouch once."

"What happen?"

Willie silently held up his left hand. Mongo had wondered what had happened to the last two fingers.

"Who chopped 'em?"

"Master," Willie sneered. "They was gonna hold me down. Ah say, 'taint no one got to hold Big Wil down." Ah struts up to that tree stump as big as day. Ah rolls up ma sleeve; an' all the time ah is rollin' it up, slow and careful, ah look at the master right in them two beady eyes of hissen. He don't say nothin . . . just keeps starin' right back. See, all the time, ah thinkin' he's fixin to take my hand. But ah had it figgered wrong. Ah lay ma hand on that block, all the time lookin' right at 'im. Then he give me a little smile and says, "Ah like you, Big Wil. You got spunk; ah think ah done change my mind.'

"With that, ah is sure he goin' to let Big Wil off. But 'stead he says, 'But you still a thief, so open that hand up and spread them fingers.' Ah did just that."

Both men were silent for some time. After awhile the neighboring planters arrived, ten or so on horseback, shouting and cursing. Mongo saw the bloodhounds on leashes, crazy to be let go, snarling and howling, and acid came up in his mouth. He saw them led to the boys' cabin where they sniffed their clothing. And then they were turned loose, nine of them, monsters bred for viciousness, running crazily around like possessed spirits until they found the scent and were off to the rocky ravine where the frolic had taken place.

Mongo listened to the discordant baying that finally subsided into silence. He and Willie went inside and ate a silent supper. Long after, when there were no sounds in the distance, Willie said that it was a good sign and grew more cheerful with each passing moment. Suddenly, he jumped up and said, "Can't lay around worryin'. We got to have some fun. Dis is Sunday."

He slapped Mongo playfully across the cheek. "Come on," he said, heading out.

Mongo got to his feet slowly and followed Willie down the hill to the second cabin from the end. They went inside. In the light of a single candle he could see the forms of sleeping people, except for the one that kneeled. Two girls sat up and rubbed their eyes. The woman kneeling looked up, and Mongo saw what the candle reflected in her moist eyes.

"What you want, Wil?" the woman asked, standing up.

"You know what ah, want, cow."

The woman's eyes widened. "What's the matter with you, Man? We all got the miseries. Naomi, she sick, frettin' for her brothers. Leave her be." She began shoving Wil toward the door.

"Who you shovin', slut," Wil shouted; and he struck her in the face, knocking her down. She lay on the floor and sobbed.

" 'Bout time you quit frettin' over them gals. Master find out what you doin' there be hell to pay. He wants them gals breedin'. Mongo here kin have Naomi. Ah's tired of her anyways. Me, ah aim to ride that youngun'. 'Bout time that little nigger was busted."

"Lawd, no, not my baby! No Wil, she too young! You hurt her sure," the mother pleaded on her knees.

"Git outta here," Wil snarled at her, " 'fore ah busts you again."

The woman, still sobbing, started to get up. Wil kicked her raised bottom and she flew through the door and landed on her face in the dirt outside.

"Cuss fire to your black heart," she cried out at him. Wil laughed. Turning toward the two girls cowering in their beds, he said, "Come here, gals. Ah wants Mongo to sees you."

The girls stood up slowly. The oldest, Naomi, was fourteen and by far the prettiest. She had known men for three years, but had never conceived. The other girl, thin and wide-eyed with fear, was much younger and a virgin.

"Ah said, come here," Wil said more sternly. They advanced a few steps.

"Naomi, this here's Mongo."

She looked up at Mongo. Any lust he had was quickly extinguished as he felt her defeated spirit and saw her sister's fear of Wil who was leering at her. Frolic time was one thing, abuse something else.

"You and Naomi go on that side," Wil said, nodding to the other end of the cabin. "Me an' the little one go to it over here." He knelt down on the mattress, putting his arms around the girl's waist, and pulled her to him. The girl tried to twist away, but Wil clutched her tightly, his face against her abdomen.

"Let her be," Mongo said quietly.

Wil looked up, surprised. "What you say?"

Mongo stood over him, feet wide. "Let her be. She too young," he said.

"Who says?" Wil pushed her away.

"Ah says."

Wil slowly got to his feet, his eyes never leaving Mongo's. They stood, two grotesque shadows in the dim light. Wil went into a slight crouch and moved slowly to his right, and Mongo waited. The assault was sudden. Wil's fist caught Mongo just over the right ear and knocked him back six feet where he slammed into the table. For a moment pain paralyzed him. Before he could recover, Wil's foot caught him in the groin; and, crazy with pain, he fell to his hands and knees. Wil was standing over him, yelling obscenely for him to get up.

Mongo gathered his strength, lunged forward, and buried his head in Wil's middle. At the same time, he grabbed Wil's legs and jerked them out from under him. Wil landed on his back with Mongo on top. Wil fought back, sinking his teeth in Mongo's wrist.

Mongo screamed in Ashantee, frantically reached out for a small stool and hammered at Wil until he lay quiet. Mongo staggered to his feet, gasping for air, and was sick to his stomach. He leaned against the table and vomited. Wil moaned and began to move around.

"You ain't hurt so bad," Mongo said; and, grabbing Wil's arm, he pulled him to his feet. "Come on, ah takes you to the cabin."

Up the hill they went, supporting each other in their misery.

Chapter Eleven

As the week passed, the tension grew. Because the boys still had not been found, each day found Ellem in an uglier mood. He cursed Martha, the house servants, and everyone who crossed his path. His years of bragging that no "nigger" had ever escaped from his place were remembered by the neighboring planters, and he became infuriated by the inference that he had finally been outsmarted by a black man.

The slightest infraction brought severe retaliation. Tom, the stable boy, was hung from the barn rafter by his wrists for not pulling the cinch on Ellem's saddle tight enough. Bess was caught putting flour into false pockets sewn into her apron and had her ear nailed to the hitching post in the front yard. She stood bent over all afternoon in the hot sun; and when the weight of her tired body finally tore the nail's head through her lobe, she took off down the road, insane with fear for having let the ear tear.

Solomon brought her back; and after supper, he and Ellem took her out to the barn and, ignoring her blood-chilling screams, clipped off both ears with a scissors.

The year was 1859. Thoughout the South planters were finding that tobacco and cotton were less profitable than breeding picaninnies. As men grew richer, the wrangling in Congress grew louder. The issue, however, was not a moral one, but whether the importation of slaves should be made legal once again. And while the bickering went on endlessly, between thirty and forty thousand slaves were being smuggled in each year from Cuba alone, many of whom were maimed and killed by their masters. And so, two great races deteriorated to something less. The southern white, lusting for personal gain, defended his acts by preaching that the Negro was inferior, as God intended him to be, and even tried to prove it with the Bible. The Negro, through suffering, intimidation, and dependence on a white master for survival, came to believe he was inferior and raised his children to believe it, also.

On the tenth day after they had run, the boys were found. The following Saturday Ellem called the planters together to demonstrate the punishment he administered to "runners" to discourage others so tempted.

He started the torture in the afternoon when the planters arrived. First, he stripped the boys, tied their hands behind them, put nooses around their heels, and hung them upside down. Tables had been set out, and brandy was served. The men lounged in the shade, drinking, while Ellem related how he had tracked the slaves into a cave down near the Mississippi.

An hour or so later, after he had repeated the story several times, he had them cut down and their hands freed. Sending for two pitchforks, he gave one to each boy.

"Now, the one that kin outdo the other gets a chance to run for his life," he said to the boys.

"What you mean, Master?" they asked, dumbfounded.

"Ah means you'uns goin' to fight to the end . . . till one kills the other."

The taller boy spoke now. "Master, this is my brother. Ah don't wants to kill 'im."

"Do you want stringin' up right now, or do you want a fightin' chance, boy?"

The boy got the message. He turned to his brother; and for awhile the two stood silently looking at each other, perhaps realizing for the first time what each meant to the other.

The planters formed a loose circle around the two and began shouting at them to begin. The house slaves watched in terror at a distance. The boys' mother and sisters came panting up the hill in time to see the boys slowly circling each other, with forks sticking out in defense.

Willie and Mongo were in a railsplitting gang up on a hill overlooking the house and could see the scene clearly.

"What's he doin' to them boys?" Mongo asked.

"Dunno," Willie answered, cupping his hand to see into the blazing sun.

They saw the boys spar with the long handled forks, and they both knew the fight was a sham. They saw Ellem go into the house with a slave and return with several hand guns and rifles. He laid them down, except for a pistol which he kept as he walked into the center of the circle. Evidently he had threatened them, for now the boys were fighting harder. The crowd closed in, blocking the view, and Mongo and Willie waited anxiously as the cheering suddenly stopped and the crowd backed away. One boy lay on his back, a pitchfork stuck through his neck and into the ground, a grotesque marker. The other boy stared down at his brother, his face grief-stricken. Suddenly, he swooped down, picked up the other fork and faced Ellem.

"Stick 'im!" Willie hissed.

"Kill 'im, kill 'im," Mongo and the other slaves joined in. Ellem slowly raised the pistol. The boy dropped his fork. Ellem stepped back and said something to the house servant who passed out weapons to the white men. Ellem lined them up facing an open field lying west of the house. The boy was escorted to the edge of the field a hundred yards away. Willie spat and kicked the yellow earth angrily.

"He goin' make 'im run."

"What you mean?" Mongo asked.

"He given' each of them one shot at the little buck. He makes it through, he's free. Favorite trick of his."

A house servant held up a handkerchief. When he dropped it, the boy took off across the field, running low as little puffs of white smoke appeared from the guns, one after another in succession. They whooped and hollered as each man tried and missed. Ellem was last in line. The boy was twenty yards from freedom. Ellem raised his rifle and took long aim at him. The planters were shouting and laughing drunkenly, hoping to make Ellem miss. Only he didn't. The puff of smoke . . . the boy tumbled to the ground. A shout went up, and some of the planters pumped Ellem's hand. He pushed them away abruptly and quickly raised the rifle. The boy was crawling on hands and knees. He was now five yards from the field's edge.

"One shot, that's all," Willie screamed. "One shot, that's all," the other man in the gang joined in the protest, shouting oaths and shaking their fists. Four yards to go. Three. The puff of smoke. The boy lay quiet.

That night there was no frolicking in the ravine, though it was Saturday. Every black man, woman, and child mourned the two brothers, and the impression Ellem had sought to make was stamped on the minds of all, except for Mongo and Willie. The hate in Mongo rose to an almost intolerable level. He confided in Willie and found that he could count on him in whatever he might attempt.

The next day being Sunday, church service was held as usual. Mongo and Willie sat in the front row again, and Mongo found himself once more intrigued with the woman in the filmy blue dress towering above him. Even his hate for Ellem, and whites in general, was softened as he listened to her quiet voice and saw the love so obvious in her face and mannerisms.

She made no reference to the recent deaths; the church service took the usual pattern. But at its conclusion she said, "Startin' this afternoon, we're going to hold special classes for any of you who wants to learn more about our Lord. All of you are welcome to come."

Though Wil tried to talk him out of it, Mongo decided to attend the meeting. To be able to see and be close to Miss Martha was an opportunity he wouldn't miss. She had been speaking for about ten minutes before he realized he hadn't heard her words. He tried to concentrate.

"You see, children, God gave Adam a free will," she

was saying. "He didn't *make* Adam love Him. Adam had a choice to love God and obey Him or not. Well, Adam decided to listen to his woman and eat the fruit. But he sinned by disobeying God, and sin has been in the world ever since."

She paused and looked over the two dozen blacks. She searched each face; and, at last, her eyes rested on Mongo. For some moments they studied each other. She asked softly, "What is your name?"

"Mongo," he answered, his temples throbbing.

"Mongo, if you were the only person on the whole earth, Jesus would still have come to die on the cross for the sins of your life." Mongo searched for the meaning to her words. The concept of sin was not new to him. At the beginning of each new season, the priest of his tribe made a sacrifice of a young goat or calf to the sun god for the sins the tribe had committed against the gods.

"Missie, this God, iffen He die for my sins, then ah got no troublement 'bout it no more."

"That is correct," she said quickly, "but he did it only for those who wants him to. Do you?"

"Sure ah wants it, why not?" he laughed, but then sobered quickly at her sincerity. He wanted to cut out his tongue. The class was terminated after a closing prayer, and Mongo returned to his cabin. He sat dejected for hours. He concluded, finally, that he could make things right by listening closer to her words.

A week went by, and it was Monday night. Mongo and Wil had worked till sundown, as usual, and were now relaxing before bedtime. Wil sat in the doorway in the path of an autumn moon. Mongo lay on his bed, head propped up on one arm. Ever since the brothers' death, Wil and he seemed to have an understanding, though neither discussed it. He was no longer watched. Wil seemed to care less if he ran or not. Matter of fact, Mongo had the notion lately that Wil was thinking of running himself.

"Wil?"

"Mmmm."

"Ever know a black man be with a white gal?"

"Huh!"

"What you mean, 'Huh'?" Mongo asked.

"Ah knows what you mean, that's 'nough." Wil swung around and looked inside the cabin at Mongo. "Best you drops it, right now. That kinda talk poison."

"Ah don't mean what you thinks. Ah mean, did you ever hear tell of a white woman lovin' a nigger?"

"No, 'cause it never happen'."

"Could happen."

"Man, you sure is ignorant. You don't know nothin'." Wil looked outside quickly to see if they were alone. "What's a white gal gonna give a nigger but troublement? Iffen they get cotched, she ain't gonna cotch nothin'. But he's goin' cotch somethin', you best believe. Listen, man, ah heard about this nigger boy one time. They say he was cotched in this young missie's bedroom. Claim he was just there, not messin' with her even. No one ever knew for sure. But you know what happen? They drug him through the town behind a hoss, and made him walk over sharp stones with his bare feet that bled like somebody done cut 'em with a knife. They never give him no water all that day and kept 'im out in the boilin' sun till they got ready to hang him. When they got ready to hang him, they put him up on a stand

and chunked rocks at his naked body. They threw gravel in his eyes and broke his ribs with big rocks. Then they put a rope around his neck and strung him up till his eyes pop out of his head. Now you tell me how a white gal kin love a nigger when all the time she knows what's bound to happen to him. You tell me."

Mongo didn't answer.

"Ah know your troublement. Man, don't you know half the niggers on this place got eyes for Missie Martha? They listen to all that stuff she preaches just to be near her. Don't you know that they know it's hopeless, so they just dream? They been told from the time they picaninnies they ain't fit to be used as steppin' stones to get her across a puddle. That's why you never see it happen." He lowered his voice. "But maybe there be a time old Wil try his luck, 'cause old Wil *know* he's a man, same as white boys, maybe even more a man."

If Wil ever tried it, Mongo knew that he would kill him.

"You be ready to run," Mongo said, sneering.

"You know that's true," Wil chuckled. "Day that happen, ah'm long gone."

Mongo chose his words. "Which way you go? The swamp?"

"Or the river, iffen I could outrun the hounds. Could do it with horses, betcha."

"Then what?"

"Ah gits an old log or anything that floats, and ah just let ol' Miss carry me along to where she will."

"Ain't you got no place special to git to?"

"Nope. Livin' on ol' Miss plenty good fo' Wil. Lots of niggers run off an' live their whole life movin' by night, sleepin' by day."

Mongo couldn't understand Wil's thinking. "How come you not head for them big boats?"

"You means down by Orleans? Never make it."

"Who says?"

"Ah says. Get caught 'fore you ever clumb up the side."

Mongo didn't agree, but he was getting sleepy, and talk suddenly seemed a chore. He stretched out and looked up at the streaks of silver dissecting the ceiling. He listened to the crickets and drifted into the first layer of sleep. As usual, he saw Miss Martha standing on the verandah in that filmy blue dress and wondered if the reason he hadn't run was really because of her. He had had a dozen opportunities, but always he had hesitated till the chance was gone. He longed to stroke that hair as light and golden as corn tassel. The last conscious thought he had was that he would do anything to have her, even take her Jesus she had urged on him and the others.

The next day he found himself working next to Gabriel, a young mulatto who sang at church meetings. They were picking corn, and Mongo soon learned the mulatto was a hard worker. It took some doing to keep up with him. The lad was highly regarded by the girls because of his lighter skin and fine features, but Mongo noticed that he never encouraged their attention. He smiled at them, but then, he was always smiling at everybody. Mongo couldn't understand how a man could be so happy. Gabriel had been humming, but now he broke into, "Oh, how I love Jesus." Then stopped and said "Hey, you wants to sing with me, ah lets you, ha!"

"Don't know them songs. Don't wants to, 'sides," Mongo muttered.

Gabriel was amazed. "Don't know how? Man, 'tain't nothin' to it! Ah'll learn you, here, listen to this..." Gabriel sang the first verse, and his clear tenor voice drifted out to the other workers; and the Christians there echoed each line all the way to the far end of the field. It was a beautiful thing to hear, but Mongo never opened his mouth. After it was over, they worked on in silence until Gabriel asked, "How come you don't sing with us, brother?"

Mongo tried to ignore the question. Finally, he stood up and wiped the sweat from his eyes. "Ah don't sing like you'uns 'cause ah don't feel like that."

Gabriel nodded his head knowingly. "Ah knows jest what you mean. Yessir, ah sure 'nough do. Was a time when ah never did much singin' neither. Had nothin' to sing 'bout, cause ah wasn't saved."

"Saved?" asked Mongo, rather belligerently. "Just what does that mean, anyhow?"

"Mean Jesus take care of you when you die," Gabriel beamed. "So livin' is easy, 'cause death ain't nothin' to be 'fraid of."

"How come you so sure? Seem to me no one know one way or the other when he die what goin' to happen." Mongo answered.

"It's hard to 'splain, but once you get saved, then you know. If you don't know, chances are you ain't saved. When ah got saved, there wasn't a doubt in my mind. Iffen ah got killed the very next minute, ah knew ah would be with the Lord."

"When all this happen...that you got yourself *saved*?"

"Seven year ago. In a jail in Orleans."

"Jail?"

"Sure enough. See, ah use to be a wench boy for a French widow that run a whorehouse. 'Long as ah did ma job, the widow use to let me run after workin'; and man did ah run! Had two other friends which masters let them run, too. We use to break into the storehouses on the wharfs and get rum and drink till daylight. Sometimes when we'd git good and liquored up we'd cotch some wench still out. We was wild all right. We'd do whatever we wants . . . thievin', rapin', drinkin'. Got worse and worse. Finally we got cotched."

"How you get cotched?"

"One of them boys got a taste for champagne. Never had none, but still he's got this cravin' that won't quit. Only place we knows to get some is this 'sclusive hotel on Market Place. We all knowed we takin' a big chance, but the vote is that we go. Nothin' else left for excitement, you might say.

"Well, we get cotched and got throwed in jail. The days goin' by and nobody comin' to get Gabe. Man, ah sits in that ole cell till my bones just achin' somethin' awful from those wet floors. Master don't know what's happen, probably don't care. They got me by maself; and ever' day this white boy comin' by to tell me the next mornin' they comin' to string me up, sure. Ah was so miserable. Then ah 'members. Ma mammy use to pray a lot when ah was a 'ninnie. So ah tried prayin'. Ah say, 'God, iffen you around someplace, which ah doubt, then please get me outa here. Ah *never* go back to that whorehouse.

"Well, nothin' happen, just like ah figured. 'Ahm thinkin' 'ahm the biggest fool ever did live. Then something very, very strange happen. Ah was sittin' and frettin' one mornin' 'bout a week later. Ah didn't know it was Sunday till this white preacher comes to ma cell door and asks me to read the Bible with him. Ah didn't even answer, just rolled over on ma side cussin' under ma breath. But he ain't leavin'. He say, 'iffen you don't care 'bout God, that's your 'fair. Iffen you don't believes it, just ask Him to wake you tonight sometimes; and when He does, ask Him to forgive you for your sins.'

"Well, ah goes to sleep; but 'fore ah do, ah say to God, 'God, iffen you care for me one little bit, then wake me up in the middle of the night to prove you are real.' Ah goes to sleep thinkin' to maself at what a fool ah am."

Gabriel took out a piece of denim and wiped his face. The two men had been working closely together, and now they casually separated as Solomon passed by on his filly. Mongo watched him, his eyes revealing his hate. Gabriel noticed it but went on with his story.

"Ah slept like a babe, but then ah is wide awake all of a sudden in the middle of the night and sweatin' up a storm, and ma cell is always cold. Ah feels so strange, man, ah didn't know what's happenin' at all. After awhile ah can't lay there no more. Ah get down on ma knees, and all of a sudden ah'm blubberin' and sobbin' lak a babe. Ah thinks 'bout the drinkin', the thievin', the rapin' ah done did: 'bout all the times ah used the Lord's name in vain, cussin' to show off, tryin' to be a big shot, always tryin' to outdo everybody. Man, ma heart was just breakin' up in little pieces with sorrowness and hurt for all the times ah kicked God in the teeth in ma life, knowin' somehow that ah had hurt Him. Ah don't know how long ah was on ma knees in that ol' cell, but then ah 'members somethin' ma mammy always said. That Jesus died for sinners, and that iffen we would clean ourselves up for Him, then we wouldn't need Him. So, raht then and there ah asked Jesus to come into ma heart; and no sooner does ah have the words out than ah knows somethin' is different. The troublement's goin' 'way, ma sorrow is turnin' sweeter and sweeter, and ah starts feelin' a peace in ma heart ah never felt 'fore in ma life. 'Fore ah knows it ah'm singin' top of ma lungs, and ah'm singin' songs ah ain't never heard 'cept when ah was a youngun'. Never was much for singin', but the Lord put the joy in ma heart that night; and I've been singin' ever since."

Mongo didn't know quite what to think. Gabriel seemed an emotional person, and this could explain a lot. Mongo had seen unstable men and women of his tribe become emotional during a ritual and have experiences they told about afterwards. But Mongo never took such stories seriously.

They worked in silence, the long black line moving through the mammoth corn crop like a wave of locusts, stripping the fall harvest and tossing the ears into wagons pulled by teams of mules that followed behind. It was hot and dry, and frequently a cry "water boy" or "take it off, boss?" was heard as the heat steadily grew worse. Mongo filled sack after sack as the morning wore on. The red dust all but suffocated him, and the horseflies bit into his back. By mid-morning there were four dropouts. Mongo had developed a habit of thinking over many things as he worked, and often whole mornings would slip by quickly. In his first days in the fields, he dwelled on different plans of escape. Then he began dreaming of Miss Martha and how it would be making love to her. But now, Gabriel's story got him thinking about his people back home, and then he thought about his two sons. He tried to calculate their ages from the time the war broke out. It had been almost two years since his capture. That would make them eleven and twelve. A shiver ran through him as he realized that they could be under bondage also, perhaps even in this country. The thought was too tormenting, and he forced his mind to other things. Doctor Bass's face flashed before him, and he wondered what had become of him. He saw forty black people pushed off the side of a ship, and their cries were so real that at one point he straightened up and looked around.

Often he thought of Tilah, though it pained him. Her love and her sacrifice were the highest human achievements he had ever known, and he was sure that Tilah was in a happy place today. He compared her faith to Gabriel's and Miss Martha's and saw little difference, in spite of all their preaching that Jesus was the only way to God.

Next, he thought about Ellem, and floods of hate ran through him as he dwelled on ways of killing him. He thought about Wil and how he might manipulate him into committing the act. He would hate to be the man who got caught doing it. He felt guilty for thinking like a coward and decided that when the time came he would do his own killing. If Wil wanted to help, that was fine. The killing itself wasn't the thing. Getting away before those four-legged demons tracked him down . . . that would be something! On a horse he might just do it. He had the escape route pretty well figured out. He had been all the way to the river with the wood cutting gangs and had memorized the terrain.

Once at the river, he would float down on anything to the outskirts of New Orleans, where he hoped to stow away on a ship bound for his country. He would know which one by the stores being loaded aboard her. He wished he knew more about the river. There was roughly twenty miles of it to travel to Orleans. He had asked Wil and some others, but no one had the information he needed.

The slaves were in a long line, walking up the steep hills to their cabins, and Gabriel was suddenly at Mongo's side. "Hey, man, Miss Martha havin' a prayer meetin' tonight after conch. You wants to come, don't make no noise. Jest go to the gully."

Mongo perked up. "Missie Martha be there?"

"Yep. Bringin' a preacher man, 'sides. Hey now, you comin'; don't let on with 'ol Wil or nobody. Master find out, we all get the devil to pay . . . Miss Martha, too. You cotch?"

"Sure 'nough," Mongo agreed.

The thought of seeing her again put new spirit in him. He was jovial through supper with Wil, who was ready to turn in after the hot day's labor.

Mongo could hardly wait for the conch horn to sound. He was sitting in the doorway and watching the cabin lights go out one by one. Wil was already snoring. The night before him was hot and black, the moon partially hidden by clouds. He was tense, his senses keenly alive to every sound and movement. He stood up and looked carefully, first to the right and then to the left, for Solomon or one of his men who walked the long row of cabins for the final check. He saw someone coming up the hill and went in and climbed into his bed. The light filled the cabin momentarily, then left, and he got up and slipped out into the night.

Chapter Twelve

"Folks, we got someone real special here with us tonight," Miss Martha began. "You cain't hardly see him, ah know; but you'll be able to hear him speak to you from the word of God and give you the latest from the North. He is Rev. Ludwig. Reverend?"

His handshake was strong, and he was smiling broadly as he moved through the fifteen or so present to greet each personally. Mongo smelled hair tonic sweetly foreign to him.

They sat down in a tight circle on the soft earth still warm from the day's sun. The preacher stood in the center and began speaking in a deep, well-enunciated northern accent.

"Brothers and sisters, it burdens me that we must meet like this; but I thank God that we can meet at all. All through the South Christians, black and white, are meeting to ask God to end bondage."

"Amen."

"Many people in the North are opposed to your suffering and are laying plans this very moment to help you. One man, you probably have heard of before, Abe Lincoln."

"Yes sir, we know him, praise God!"

"He is getting much public support. I have it on first-hand knowledge that he is a Christian. He accepted our Savior as a young man; and in a creed he has written, he said that the Bible is the best gift God had ever given to men."

"Amen."

"Praise God for Mr. Lincoln."

Mongo saw yellow hair reflect the timid moon.

"As for myself, I was saved at nine years of age but didn't really start living for the Lord till I was sixteen. God has sent me far and wide to encourage folks to cling to Him and His word no matter what circumstances they are in. A man may chain your body, but he can't chain your soul."

"Amen."

"Tell it, Preacher."

"He may whip you, tear your limbs out, even kill you; but he can't harm your soul. Not if you've already given that to God."

"Yes, praise the Lord."

"If you belong to the Lord, you should live the kind of life the apostle Paul writes about."

"Amen, Preacher."

"That means you stay out of the master's henhouse."

"Amen."

"That means you leave other people's women alone."

"Yeah, man!"

"That means you do whatever your master tells you to do."

Silence.

"A lot of preachers are preaching today that black people don't have souls . . . that they're just like hogs or cattle . . . that this life is the only one you'll ever have . . . that when you die, you're thrown into a hole and there isn't a hereafter for you. Well, I'm here to tell you that that isn't true! The word of God says that everyone has a soul that will go on living after death, either in heaven or hell."

Emotion welled up in Mongo like an approaching storm. He longed to embrace Martha even at the risk of death. The pastor was more somber now. "Let me ask you all a question. How many of you know exactly where your soul would go if you died tonight?"

Hands went up all around. Except Mongo's.

The preacher didn't seem to notice. "You know, a man said one time you can't really start living until you're no longer afraid to die."

"Amen!"

"You said it!"

"I'm sure glad I'm saved!"

"Can I ask you somethin'?" Mongo blurted, more to get Martha's attention than anything.

"By all means," the preacher said, turning his way.

"Seems to me there ain't no diff'rence 'tween your God and the gods ma people worship in ma country. God is God. Some calls Him this or that, but He don't care. 'Portant thing is that a man be right with hisself. Then everything turn out fine in the end. Betcha." It was a new concept to many of them, and they were all staring.

"Yes, I know a lot of people think that way; but I don't believe it's enough for salvation of the soul. Jesus came for a reason. Throughout the Bible we are told that there is no salvation outside of Him. He, Himself, said, "I am the way, the truth, and the life; no man cometh unto the Father but by me.' If you can make it to heaven outside of Jesus, you would be a witness through all eternity that Jesus Christ was a liar. I won't call Him that. Will you?"

Mongo puzzled over the question. Then he said, "You mean all the people back home an' in other lands will be lost when they die 'cause they didn't know this Jesus?" He was beginning to enjoy confronting this fancy white man.

"We know that God is just," the preacher answered. "We can believe that His dealings with all people will be fair. I don't believe He will condemn a man for rejecting a Christ he has never heard about; but, rather, the man will be condemned for violating his own moral standard. But there's something else we must consider here. Scripture points out that there is enough evidence in the universe to prove to every man that the true God of creation does exist. Romans 1:19-20 says: 'For what can be known about God is plain to them, because God has shown it to them. Ever since the creation of the world his invisible nature, namely his eternal power and deity, has been clearly seen in the things that have been made. So they are without excuse.' "

"Ma people always seekin' the light back home," Mongo said. "Some of them prayin' all day and half the night. Nobody tole them nothin' 'bout Christ."

"But to whom do they pray?"

"To they gods. Same as you."

"And who are their gods?"

"Well, there's a god for any which thing you wants one for. There's a god of rain, a god of fire. Ever' one got one he likes best. Then he take a hunk of mangrove an' whittle away till he make somethin' he like."

"You mean he creates an idol?"

"Yessir, but they call it god."

"Then what?"

"Then he just prays."

"To the idol?"

Mongo hesitated. He was being drawn into a troublesome position.

"Yes," he answered, not knowing what else to say.

"When you have prayed to an idol, have you found this a satisfying experience?"

There it was. But how to deal with it? His thoughts flashed back to the long, tedious rituals he had been a part of as a young warrior. He had always come away with the same emptiness until he stopped it altogether when he and Tilah began raising a family. He had never faced this issue before, but he could not admit to this stranger and the others that this had been a problem for him.

"He can't answer that, Preacher, 'cause he knows it ain't so," said an old man whose white hair stood out in the darkness and who was probably the oldest field hand on the place. "Ah did a lot of idol prayin' back home, same as this young buck. One time ma brother an' me carves us a war god. Iffen we ain't fightin', we prayin' to our god; and iffen we ain't prayin', we fightin'. One day, after a fight we had, ah'm kneelin' with ma nose in the dirt when ah thinks all this prayin' we been doin' ain't helpin' us at all, seein' as though ma head is been laid wide open from a lance and my brother's innards is all but hangin' out of him. Ah gits up out of the dirt, and ah walks outside and looks up at the sky and the tall trees with vines trailin' down, covered with flowers the size of a wagon wheel. Ah looks out over the hills covered with tall grass ripplin' like waves on the ocean as far as ah can see, and ah wonders how a god carved from wood kin have anything to do with all this wonderment 'round me. And deep down, ah knew it wasn't so. Ah looked up at the sky, stretched out ma arms, and cried, 'God of this creation, the one who made all this, ah craves to know you.''

The old man paused as he tried to handle the emotion that began to seep into his voice. Mongo and the others waited expectantly.

"Ah quit prayin' to idols after that day and began to talk to a God ah was sure was there. One year later ah had nary a doubt he lived even when he put me in bondage. Ah lost my family when ah comes here. Oh, how ah grieved for 'em. But the day ah heard Missie Martha talk about Jesus ah knew raht then an' there why he put me into bondage. It was so's ah could come here and accept His Son and be saved, and for this ah praise Him mightily.''

"Praise God!"

"Amen."

Silence. Mongo knew they were waiting for him to react to this testimony. The old man's acceptance of his bondage disgusted him. Still, Mongo had a fleeting urge to lay down his weapons, to admit he might be wrong and go on learning from there. But his pride stopped him. A chill ran through him as he wondered if he might really be lost. Threatened now, he lashed back.

"Iffen this Jesus is so lovin' and all, then how come he put us all under yoke? And how come he 'lowed them two brothers get killed, and how 'bout all them younguns get themselves carved up ever time a village gets raided? What about ma Tilah and ma boys an' . . .!" His voice rose to a frantic pitch; and when he stopped for breath, he noticed for the first time that many had bowed their heads and closed their eyes.

For a long time it was very quiet, except for the owl and a cricket's serenade. Mongo just sat there, the battle raging within him, feeling very alone.

Chapter Thirteen

After a few testimonies and two or three quietly sung songs, Reverend Ludwig closed the meeting with a prayer, and the group headed quietly up the hill in twos and threes. Mongo, his composure regained, waited for Martha, the last in line.

"Miss Martha," he said softly, falling in beside her. "Be a great pleasure iffen you allow Mongo to help you up the hill."

Martha was pleased. She hoped to water the seed planted by the Reverend.

About halfway up, they came to a brook, and when Martha hesitated, Mongo gently slipped one arm around her, picked her up, and carried her across. He set her down, but not before he made her look him in the eyes. At once, she was aware of musk scent and hard muscles. A very slight twinge of excitement flittered through her.

He helped her once more when she slipped before they reached the top; immediately, little shocks pricked her, and she began to wonder at herself. Wistfully, she began thinking of romantic high points in her life: her first kiss, her wedding night, those early days of lovemaking with Dan Ellem, until she later built a wall to contain her inner drives when he began to treat her little better than one of his black wenches.

At the top stood a sycamore tree; when they reached it, Mongo stopped and tugged at Martha's sleeve.

"Miss Martha, ah craves to tell you somethin'."

"Yes, Mongo?" Martha said.

"Miss Martha, them other boys call themselves 'niggers'. Do you think of me that way?"

"No, Mongo, I don't approve of that expression. God made all men equal."

Mongo was encouraged. "Miss Martha, do you think the day comin' when black men and white gals jump over the broom?"

"Mongo, on this place a man and woman are married by a minister of God. Jumpin' over a broom is a heathen custom!"

"You didn't answer ma question," Mongo said firmly.

"Yes, Mongo, that day will come."

"When?"

"Oh, it may take years, many years. Why?"

Mongo gently took her hand and held it in both of his. " 'Cause ah loves you Miss Martha; ah wants you go run away with me."

She was so shocked she giggled self-consciously at first, but then she was laughing. "Mongo, you don't mean that!" she was able to say finally. "You're just lonely and homesick for your family."

But Mongo was starting up the hill.

Sobering quickly, she scampered after him. When she finally caught up and touched his shoulder, he whirled and snarled, "What you wants with me? You got your Jesus." He shoved her away and continued up the hill.

Martha was crying when she arrived at the big house.

Slipping off her shoes, she tiptoed through the kitchen door, left unlocked so the kitchen help could get in to start the breakfast fires early. She made her way through the kitchen across the dining room to the front staircase. Finding the big banister in the darkness, she used it to wearily pull herself up the stairs to the second floor.

By mutual agreement, Martha and Ellem slept in separate rooms, each at opposite ends of the long hallway. Old Ben, Ellem's half-deaf body servant, slept in a smaller room next to his master's. No other servants slept on the second floor. She found her room easily at the top of the stairs, made her way in, closed the door quietly, and slipped the bolt. Choosing not to risk light, even though she was sure Ellem was sleeping soundly from all the peach brandy he had consumed at dinner, she undressed by the light of the moon coming through the huge French window. Her room was hot, even though a cool breeze was puffing the filmy curtains. She stood before the open window and let the breeze caress her bare body.

She stood there trying to sort out her emotions. Why did she feel so badly? Was it because he had rejected her? Why should that bother her so? She wouldn't dare let herself even begin to admit that she had any romantic feelings for him, but one thing was sure. She had hurt him. How could she have been so insensitive?

Suddenly, she was aware that she was not alone. She heard someone breathing immediately behind her just before her wind was cut off by an arm around her throat. A rag was forced into her mouth, making her gag. Then, what felt like a burlap bag was forced over her head. She fell to her hands and knees and screamed, but the sounds were that of a mute. She tried to tear off the bag which threatened to suffocate her, but her hands were roughly tied behind her back.

She was picked up and thrown to the floor on her back. Aware now of her attacker's intent, she began kicking out with her feet and trying to keep her thighs together at the same time. Then she was struck on the head and lost consciousness.

Little Jesse found her in the morning and screamed so loud that everyone in the house, including Ellem, came running. Martha tried to answer his questions coherently, but she could shed little light on who her attacker had been. Yes, he was a slave. She was fairly sure from the musty scent. He was big and powerful. No, he hadn't said anything. Yes, she had screamed, screamed until her head exploded.

Ellem was more furious at this outrage against *his wife* than he was concerned with her condition. He stormed out and had all hands "conched" in from the fields.

Thirty minutes later they stood before him, a trembling, pitiful humanity. They knew about Miss Martha already, and most of them grieved for her. Roll was taken; everyone was present. Ellem strutted up and down before the long line with his riding whip slapping his boot or the flanks of someone he happened to be near.

"Iffen anyone even got a sniff who did this dastardly

act, then he or she better speak out; cause iffen they don't, and iffen ah don't find out who done it . . . ah aim to castrate ever' buck on this here place."

The long line stood deathly silent. Ellem's sincerity was not doubted. He would surely do it. Ellem continued pacing back and forth, like a disturbed wasp, ready to attack at the slightest provocation. Behind him stood Solomon and a newly-hired backup white named Charlie. All three whites were armed with colt revolvers stuck in their belts.

Mongo stood very rigid, midway down the line. Big Wil stood at his right. Mongo never took his eyes off Ellem, but he was aware that those nearest were watching him. He had been the last to be seen with Miss Martha. Fear was rampant. It could be seen in the nervous gestures and expressions. One remark or motion toward him and he could be dead.

"Git the slaughter knife, Sol," Ellem barked. "Ah ain't lolligaggin' 'round here all day."

Solomon left to get the hog-butchering cleaver. Ellem ordered two slaves to take the first man in line and bring him to a large stump nearby which appeared tailor-made for Ellem's gruesome object lesson. The man was wide-eyed with terror but made no sound.

Ellem took the cleaver from Solomon and held it up high. "You got two minutes."

Solomon and Charlie had their pistols out. The slaves were beginning to react along the line. Some fidgeted; some just stared in open-mouthed terror; and some wept.

"All right, that's it. This be your last chance. What's it goin' to be? A plantation of freaks, or one man payin' for his crime?"

Silence. Horseflies buzzing. Unattended picaninnies squalling in the cabins. Crows holding court somewhere deep in the woods. A woman, very white, lies on her sheets and listens to the voice beneath her in the yard and prays desperately. The cleaver starts its journey upward, and all eyes watch, mezmerized.

"Master."

All heads turned to see Gabriel step out from the line.

"Well?"

"Ah'm your man."

"That right?"

"Yes sir."

"Come here."

The mulatto tenor moved obediently to arm's length of his master.

"Why, Gabe?"

Gabe swallowed hard. "Ah hankered."

"You hankered a white woman?" Ellem's face twisted into ugly disbelief.

"Yes sir."

"Knowin' what happens to niggers tech a white woman?"

"Yes sir."

"Enjoy it?"

Gabriel stared at the ground, not answering. The whip lashed his right cheek. He went to his knees and held his face with both hands, the tears streaming to the red earth.

"Git up, nigger." Gabe got to his feet very slowly.

"Should have knowed it to be a Christian hypocrite," Ellem sneered to his seconds. "Who else?"

"Sir?"

"Ah said, who else?" Ellem repeated, impatiently.
"No one, sir."
"You lyin', and it goes double hard fo' you."
"Weren't nobody else, Master," Gabe looked into Ellem's eyes. "Ah swore."

Ellem studied the young mulatto, then ordered that he be tied hanging upside down, spread eagled, and castrated. As the slaves were ordered back to work, he was left hanging upside down while the blood ran down his body and off the tip of his nose till he was dead; but they couldn't take him down. And all the while they knew he was innocent.

Mongo lay in his bunk that night, listening to Gabe's moaning that had long ceased, and he tried to put things together. He was aware there were more than a few slaves who thought he should have been strung up with feet to the sky. He dared not sleep, but lay there fondling a heavy oak table leg he kept hidden in his bunk. He had gone over his list of likely suspects the third time when he realized there was only one black man on the place with enough gumption to have committed the act. Big Wil snored loudly across the room.

He got up and tiptoed to a chair with Wil's shirt draped over it. He picked it up and sniffed it. There was the strong body odor, but there was more. He could smell cologne that he knew was Miss Martha's. He fought down an urge to get the table leg and cave in Wil's skull. He stood, instead, and stared down at the sleeping form for a long time. When he turned to climb back into his bunk, the words, "You are a dead man," disrupted the silence of the tiny cabin.

The next day in the field, Mongo stayed close to Big Wil. Wil was quiet as usual, and Mongo could discover nothing out of the ordinary in his actions. Slowly, monotonously, the days dragged on. Miss Martha was holding church services once again, but she was not herself. She had lost weight and color and did not speak with the same enthusiasm. He tried to approach her after the services, but she wouldn't look at or speak to him. Mongo was torn by her rejection and the knowledge that he was still suspected by everyone to have been the cause of her change. And so, night after night, he tossed tormentedly on his mattress, vowing that at the right moment, perhaps at woodcutting time when "accidents" often happened, Big Wil's act would be repaid.

Chapter Fourteen

Martha sat at her window and gazed at the multi-colored western sky. Soon the sun would set for another day. It was her favorite time of day, her favorite time of year, autumn with its majestic color scheme, but these things only faintly moved her now. Since the night of the attack, she had retreated into another world.

At first, she met the issues straight on. God had allowed a painful thing to happen to her. She was sure He had a purpose. But why had He taken Gabriel's life? She knew Mongo was innocent, because her attacker had reeked from alcohol, and Mongo had not minutes earlier. She prayed and prayed, but the hurt and loneliness remained.

Thoughts of Mongo's words to her that night were with her constantly, easing the loneliness and rejection she felt from everyone on the plantation, especially Ellem and the overseers. She knew Mongo was hurting. For his own safety, she had avoided him at the church services, but now, she felt a growing compulsion to tell him she knew he was innocent.

She began to devise a plan that would permit a clandestine meeting, and all the time she planned fear never left her. She could remember, as a young girl only two years married, how she had let herself become mildly flirtatious with a handsome slave buyer traveling through at a party to which Ellem had taken her.

Ellem had beat her. She forgave him for the cursing and names he called her as he flung her around the room. Oh, but the real pain came afterwards when she heard him sneak out the kitchen door to the cabins down the hill.

She found herself going to God often as Ellem continued to abuse and use her in the ensuing years, and it always helped. Now her loneliness, stronger than fear, more powerful than her feelings for God, seemed to carry her along like a chip on the ocean, a victim of stormy emotion. She was like a man drowning with a sack of gold in each hand. Hers was black gold: Mongo.

It was dark now. Soon conch would sound. She went to her vanity, found a very special perfume, and applied it to her body. Quietly, she slipped down the stairs and out the back door.

He was waiting exactly where she had directed in the note carried by her trusted Jesse. He was sitting on a stump, head in hands. When he heard her, he jumped up and moved toward her.

"Miss Martha?" he asked, softly.

"Yes, it's me," she answered.

They touched for a moment, then Martha sat down on a log. For a long while neither spoke. Both wanted desperately to answer the needs they sensed in the other, but because of the great risk, they parted shortly. A week later they met again and said many things that helped ease the pain each felt. The third time when they met and were about to part, Mongo said, "Miss Martha, there's something ah craves to say to you."

"What, Mongo?"

"Run away with me," he said, tensely.

This time she didn't laugh. His arms were around her, caressing her gently. Though her need to be loved was acute, she pulled away. "Mongo, don't you know how senseless that would be? My husband . . ."

"Been thinkin' 'bout him," Mongo hissed. "Been thinkin' 'bout all the hurt he's caused. 'Bout how he been mean to you. Sometimes ah get worked up so bad ah can hardly stand it. Ah think 'bout that boy crawlin' across that field. Ah see him drop a hundred times. Then ah see Ellem and that hog cleaver he used on Gabe in ma head."

"No!" Martha gasped.

"Got to be. The others give up one, two days. But not him. He never give it up till he cotch us."

"Mongo, if you care about me at all, you must promise me you will not even think about such a thing."

Martha turned away, searching desperately for an answer. Dimly, she was beginning to realize her folly. Because of her a man would be killed, even though it was a man she no longer loved. She knew she had gotten out of bounds, and suddenly, wanted very much to make it all right.

"Mongo, how could ah care for a man that would murder?"

"What's he got you? The way he treats you, you don't love him. Ain't that the truth?"

"Ah don't know the truth anymore," she sighed.

"Ah've been trying to hide from the truth but . . . ah guess ah really knew it would be a matter of time. How we deceive ourselves! And all the time God waits patiently. And then one day, He raises a little finger ever so slightly and everything turns upside down. And there we stand, all exposed."

For a while neither spoke. Then Mongo said, "Iffen ah doesn't kill him, will you still meet me like this?"

She took a deep breath. She needed help for this impossible task.

"Mongo, dear. We are runnin' a fool's race. You know you could lose your life. Ah couldn't live out ma life, knowin' it had been 'cause of me. Do you hear what ah'm sayin'?"

"Yes, and ah don't care. What ah got to live for? They took ma woman, ma boys, took me in chains to be a slave. You come into ma life, and ah start feelin' like ma old self . . . like a man can hold his head high. You did that for me. You did that, and ah thanks you."

They listened to an owl in the distance, and after a while she said softly, "Do you believe in God, Mongo?"

"Ah don't know. Many times ah sit and think and wonder. Ah thinks 'bout life and how did it start. Ah think 'bout love, how powerful it is. Ah thinks 'bout how much ah loves you, and ah say to maself that your love is all ah need. But . . ." he paused for a moment, "ah knows there's got to be somethin' else. Where did this all begin?" He looked up at the star-filled heavens.

"Ah means, ah have seen men who have got somethin'. Whatever it is, it spills out and touches you. Ah saw it in a doctor on a boat. Ah saw it in some of ma people here. Ah saw it in you and in a pretty boy that had so much of it his life was nothin' to him. What is it?" He looked at her, expectantly, suddenly without pride or arrogance.

"It is God that you have seen, Mongo," she said softly. "Some folks know God, really know Him. They have met Him and live to please Him. He uses them to reach others. His love shines through them and draws like a magnet; and just as Jesus promised, they become fishers of men. Their net is His love."

He was listening carefully, putting another piece into a lifetime puzzle, each piece representing a person like Doctor Bass aboard the Zong, or the Creek Indian, or Gabe. He wanted that kind of love very badly.

"Miss Martha," he whispered, pulling her to him, "come with me tonight; be ma woman."

Martha pulled away. "No, Mongo, ah cannot. As much as ah care, ah can't. We would not be happy. We'd never stop running. Mongo, try to understand..."

He didn't want to *understand*.

He began to pace. "Ah guess ah knew it was comin'. How could you love me, a common nigger. I'm not a man in your eyes; I'm a heathen."

"Mongo, don't, please."

"Well, it's true. You see me as a heathen slave you got to change to your way of thinkin'. Long as I say the right words, you're happy." He knew he was hurting her, but he couldn't stop. "Just like everyone else 'round here. They know what you wants to hear. The joke is, everyone knows it but you. 'Nother thing..."

She couldn't listen to any more. She stumbled back along the path to the big house.

Long after she had gone, he stood leaning against a tree sobbing, heart and soul torn open, leaving only ugliness in place of beauty, bitterness in place of the love he had felt earlier.

Each night he went to their secret place, but she did not return. Within a week he was in the "rack" twice for sassing Solomon. The almost-healed wounds of long ago began festering til they became open sores. He spent his days sulking, his nights having nightmares of vengeance against Ellem or Solomon, or the other overseers, for wrongs committed against himself or his people.

Martha had gone. Unknown to everyone except her husband, he had allowed her a vacation with her sister, Jamie, who lived in an adjoining county, for a "change of scenery." This further tormented Mongo as he came to the conclusion that Ellem had sent her away. The more he dwelled on it, the bigger monster Ellem became. Each day in the field grew shorter, as he spent most of it deep in thought. He had now definitely decided to run, since his pride would allow him no other recourse. But he would not run with panic as his companion, and though he knew Martha would never forgive him, he knew that he would kill Ellem. There was a man hanging spread-eagled and a boy crawling across a field whenever he closed his eyes; and he knew that when the time came, the instrument of destruction would be a certain broad cleaver about fourteen inches long and about eight inches wide, with a sweeping edge much worn by cutting into the members of hogs, and at least one black man.

He would go alone if need be, but it would be better to have help. He didn't want to accept it, but the only black with the knowledge he needed, or the guts to kill whites, was Big Wil. Later, there would be time to fulfill his vow.

When he had everything worked out, he waited for the appropriate time to make the approach. One night after supper, two weeks prior to Christmas, Wil seemed more amiable than usual. Organizing his words for effectiveness, Mongo went into action.

"Man, ah sure 'nough gettin' ma fill of this hog slop," he growled, slamming his half-eaten plate of corn meal mush on the table.

"We gettin' better'n some," Wil answered.

"Huh."

"You always belly-achin' 'bout somethin' lately. Seems to me you quit belly-achin' and do somethin' iffen you don't like it," Wil taunted.

"Aim to," Mongo said as matter-of-fact as he could. Wil looked up and studied him. "You been thinkin', man?"

"Could be."

Silence.

"What you been thinkin'?"

"Now don't go get yourself all conjured up." Mongo stretched out on his mattress, sighing contentedly. Knowing Wil was watching, he closed his eyes as if to turn in. Wil went to the wooden pail hanging on a nail and drank from a green gourd dipper. He stood in the doorway, looking out, then came back and sat down on his own mattress.

"Been doin' some thinkin' maself," he announced. Mongo feigned sleep. "Hey, you listenin'?"

Mongo forced a response. "What you want with me? Can't you let a body get some sleep?"

"You goin' run?" Wil leaned forward eagerly.

Mongo drew himself up on one elbow and squinted at Wil for a long moment as if he were gauging his trustworthiness. "What ah do is ma 'fair." He lay back down.

"Sure 'nough."

Silence.

"You goin' do him in?" Wil whispered hungrily.

More silence.

"Do *who* in?"

"Ah wants to go with you," Wil blurted out.

"Huh."

"You goin' need help. You can't do it yourself, betcha."

"Who says?"

"Ah says."

Silence.

"Have it your way, then," said Wil. " 'Ceptin', ah knows things you don't. Things you got to know on the run."

Silence. Now it was Wil's turn to play possum as he lay down with his face to the wall. Mongo waited a few minutes, then said, "What you know?" He paused. "Iffen ah do let you in, ah'm the boss, right?"

"Right."

"Ah mean, ah got a plan with a heap of thinkin' in it. Don't need more. But ah do need someone ah can trust. Kill iffen ah says so and when ah says so."

"Right."

"Ah know you can talk, but ah don't know iffen you can kill."

"Ah can kill. Slow, quick, whatever."

"Once we off, that's it. We ain't never comin' back, leastways, not live and kickin'."

"Right."

"We head south to Orleans and them big boats."

"How you get on the boat?"

"Worry 'bout that when the time comes," Mongo said confidently. "Now, what you know 'bout the river? How long it take to make Orleans?"

"Two days, iffen we just let ol' Miss carry us by night and hide out the day."

"What can you get? We need hosses, victuals, matches, knives, a hoss pistol . . ."

"Lemme think on it. No troublement, 'cept the pistol. When we goin'?"

"Christmas night."

"During the frolic time?"

"After."

"Hey now, you got somethin' there. Ever' one be double-eyed with spirits."

"Ever' one, 'ceptin' them devil hounds," said Mongo. Wil studied Mongo's implication.

"You know a way to outthink 'em?" Mongo asked.

Wil nodded negatively. "They smell too good, run too fast for a nigger. Lessen we poison them."

"Thought of that. There was seven last time ah counted. We can get them okay, but them other planters have a whole mess down on us from all 'round. 'Member the time them two little bucks run?"

"Ah 'members. But least we get an hour or two head start."

Both thought a while, then Wil whispered, "How you do him in?"

"Slow . . . his way. Watch 'im, catch 'im in a cabin all liquored up with Bess or some other slut. Can't hurt the woman . . . be careful . . ." He was half talking to himself, as though he were repeating the same words for the thousandth time.

The next two weeks were the most trying in Mongo's memory. He knew sleep was important for the ordeal ahead, but each night he tossed on his mattress. They were able to steal corn meal and bacon from the kitchen storeroom the third night after he and Wil had talked, but they had some trouble locating the cleaver till Mongo found it hanging on a nail in the barn along with a corn shucker. Luckily, he found a stone for honing both knives to hair-splitting sharpness. When he was satisfied with the cleaver, he squared off on a piece of stovewood and split it expertly in two.

Christmas on a Southern plantation was looked forward to with much pleasure by black people. It meant a new shirt, or a plug of tobacco and hunk of turkey, or cow belly at dinnertime, and maybe, if they had been especially deserving, some sour cider at the frolic.

Martha had returned and was busily engaged in the many details necessary to make Christmas meaningful for the slaves. She spun extra clothes for the families of Gabe and the two brothers. She had little time to think of Mongo, but when she did, she said a short prayer like, "Father, watch over him, draw him to thee, and Father, please remove me from his thoughts." In this way was she able to control her desires for him that she knew, if left unchecked, could only destroy.

Chapter Fifteen

December 25, 1860, marked the close of a hard-fought election year. Lincoln was nominated by the Republicans and managed to defeat Breckinridge, Douglas, and Bell for the presidency, marking the beginning of the secession of the states. Two months later the Confederacy was to be formed; and two months after that, on April 12, 1861, Fort Sumpter was fired upon, beginning the "war of secession."

There was no question in anyone's mind that Louisiana would follow South Carolina's example and secede with the other slaves states. People only wondered when. War was not openly discussed, only hinted at; and Ellem's guests this Christmas day did not feel threatened by the gathering war rumors. They had had a good year financially. Following Ellem's example of two years earlier, they had all gone over to breeding, buying and selling blacks; and the market had held, yielding large profits.

Now the planters and their wives lounged around a huge oak coffee table in the drawing room, drank hot toddies served by "fancy" boys dressed in white satin for the occasion, and peered at each other through the thick smoke of the men's imported Cuban cigars.

As usual, Ellem was monopolizing the conversation. "Tell you what ah think about this whole situation. 'Iffen ah had sat on that jury, that Brown would have been made more of an example than just a hangin'! Ma daddy always said hangin' was for civilized men, not for the likes of him. Him ah would have hung upside down in the town square, like they do the niggers in Cuba. Ever' passerby gets to stick his whittlin' knife into him, and his missus, her hat pin," Ellem said, nodding to the ladies. All of them seemed to be quite interested, except Martha who sat looking down at her hands folded in her lap.

"Or burn 'em like they do the niggers in Georgia," interjected a planter.

"Right," agreed Ellem with vigor. "Ah heard tell them Northern abolitionists are callin' him a martyr. Can you 'magine! By his own words he meant to get the niggers of Harper's Ferry to insurrect and burn the houses of the whites and kill off every last man, woman, and child. They claim he was a Bible toter, which explains a lot, to ma way of thinkin'." He glared at Martha and smiled at her embarassment.

"It sure do worry my bones when I think of somethin' akin happenin' in these parts," said a pert widow about thirty whose long hair had prematurely turned a beautiful silver-gray.

"Ma'am, don't fret yourself none," Ellem chided, enjoying her partially bared bosom and considering what the possibility might be later in the evening. "Them niggers didn't rally 'round Brown at Harper's, and they won't 'round here."

The widow read his suggestive message and returned it.

"That's a point," the others agreed wholeheartedly.

"Time for renourishment. Boy!" shouted Ellem, who had suddenly become quite animated. "Get in here and tend to these guests." The boy, who had momentarily left to reheat his pitcher, came running and quickly filled everyone's glass, except Martha's.

As the evening slipped by, Martha tried to ignore the eyeplay between her husband and the widow and concentrate on the needs of the guests. But later, when it had become very obvious, she asked to be excused, pleading a headache.

Meanwhile, down at the big barn a peculiar people with a peculiar talent for enjoying themselves frolicked, clapped hands, rolled their eyes at each other and laughed as though they hadn't a care in the world. Solomon and Charlie sat in one corner of the barn sharing a jug and kept an eye out that things didn't get too rowdy. At the last minute, Ellem had decided to let the slaves into the cider, and a barrel stood in the corner and was constantly being attacked by green gourd dippers. Outside, where the hounds were penned some distance away, three lay dying from having eaten rabbit floured in rat poison.

By midnight the plantation was silent. Ellem's guests had all been assigned their rooms, and most were asleep. The frolic, which ended quietly when the cider gave out, was already a dream to be stored for the hard days ahead. Solomon and Charlie, too relaxed to care about taking night check, were turning in in the cabin they shared behind the big house.

The night air had turned crisp and humid. Clouds were gathering to the west and partially obliterated the moon, making the night very dark. Oddly, the usual sounds of life in the woods were missing. For moments, the world seemed to hang motionless and wait. And watch. It watched the lights that went out one by one in the guest rooms on the second floor of the big house. It waited for a man to come out of the house and make his way to the cabins for carnal pleasures; and three hours later, it still waited.

"He ain't comin'."

"Shhh."

"Something's happenin' in there."

"Come on, let's forget him."

"You know better."

"Listen, man, daylight comin'."

"That's right, daylight comin'."

"Don't mock me, man."

"Shhh, ah hear somethin'."

Down at the pens one of the dying hounds howled sorrowfully, then was silent.

"Damn dogs get us cotched yet."

The waiting was eternal. Finally, Wil could stand it no longer.

"That's it, man, that's it." He jumped up. "Ah'm gettin' the hell outer here."

Mongo got to his feet. "Ok, we goin' in."

"In the house?"

"In the house."

"With all them peoples in there? You crazy."

Mongo grabbed Wil by the shirt front and yanked him forward. "Iffen ah'm crazy then what are you, chicken? Your black ass hangin' out, you know that?"

"What you mean?"

"Ah mean you got a chance tonight to give a whole heap of folks in their graves some peace, iffen you man 'nough, which ah doubted from the firstest. Your troublement is you a black-ass, just like all them other niggers. Someday you goin' find out you a man firstest, black-assed secondest!"

The words were like the hiss of a rattle snake. Mongo's spittle hitting Wil in the face might as well have been venom. Wil bristled. He stood wiping away the spittle, knowing it was true, that he had somehow lost much of the pride that a long time ago had allowed him to walk up to a tree stump and contemptuously roll up his shirt sleeve to have a limb chopped off. But the deep hate he had felt that had given him strength that day suddenly blazed in his memory, and drawing himself up, he took a deep breath and was changed once more into something that was anything but "black-assed". "Let's go," he said.

Even though they were fifty yards from the house, they tiptoed stealthily across the back yard. They paused every so often and listened. One of the horses they had tied behind the barn whinnied once, freezing them for a long time. They were barefooted, and their steps were silent as they made their way up the back stairs and across the big porch. Mongo paused there, put the cleaver under an arm, and wiped his sweating palms on his trousers. Then he took the cleaver's wet handle and wiped it under his arm.

"Don't hit nothin' with that big knife when you go through the house," he whispered. But as he started to open the screen door, the first wave of apprehension hit him. He had been in the house on two occasions, but in the dark he couldn't be sure of its inner workings.

"Listen," he said, "you recollect the inside?" remembering bitterly that of course Wil would know.

"Just follow. Ah takes you through," Wil said.

"Ellem's room down the other end when we get upstairs, right?" This Mongo remembered from conversation with the house servants.

"Right." Wil thought a moment. "Hey, ah just recollect. Jesse told me the other day since Missie Martha got jumped, Master got hisself a new hound up to stay there with him."

Mongo froze. "Where?" he asked, hoarsely.

"Dunno. Up top of them stairs, somewheres."

Terror raced through Mongo, icy, acid-tasting, paralyzing. He saw demon-like monsters in his mind, crazy to be let go to hunt down and kill, and he could not erase the picture. Wil was waiting. Mongo felt the streams of perspiration run down his jaw; and he wondered if Wil could see him in the darkness.

"What you waitin' on?" Wil asked, but then, sensing Mongo's dilemma, hissed, "Haw, who's black-assed now?"

The words cut into Mongo like the lash from a bull whip. He wiped his face with his sleeve and shook his head to clear it. He grabbed the door handle determinedly and opened the door slowly. Wil slipped in ahead of him. They moved stealthily along the outer wall of the kitchen, through the hallway along the bottom of the giant staircase and stopped at the foot of the stairs. In the blackness they could just make out the outline of the stairs at the top. Mongo took the lead now and stepped up two stairs at a time, deliberately, cat-like, using every bit of skill he learned stalking prey in the jungle. When he moved, Wil moved, and when he put his foot down he applied the pressure very gradually, and the squeaks from the old stairs were barely audible. He did not hurry, but listened for a moment after each move. When he was at the top, he paused. He could see down the hallway in both directions. It was very quiet. Dim, flickering light shone from underneath several of the doors which, he concluded, came from the fireplaces that had been lit to remove the chill for the guests. The demon was not in the hallway. His relief was so great he felt himself go rubbery for an instant. He took a deep breath and let the air out slowly.

With Wil on his heels, moving only when he moved, he started down the long hallway. His eyes never left that massive door at the far end that marked the master bedroom, and he hugged the wall every step, alert to every sound. He paused again, but could hear nothing. When he reached the huge door, he paused and rested against the wall, trying to gather strength from its rough stucco surface. Carefully, he changed the cleaver to his left hand and wiped his sweating palm against his trousers. He took the big brass knob and ever so slowly tried to turn it. He withdrew his hand and tried to think. He tried the knob once more, but this time he turned it in the opposite direction and felt it give. A light puff of air caressed his cheek as the door shivered a little and broke loose. He opened it just enough to get his head through. The light from the dying coals of the fireplace revealed a figure in the bed. He opened the door a bit more and slid through sideways. He felt the carpet under his bare feet and was grateful. Holding Wil at the door, he tip-toed to the head of the bed. The sleeper's form, buried deep in the feather mattress, was completely covered by a thick feather comforter, including the head.

He started to raise the cleaver when a movement caught his eye. He made out a shadow poised in the open doorway of the adjoining privy. The shadow stood quite still as Mongo waited. Like distant thunder, the growl began, low and deep; then the bloodhound began to slink forward on its belly toward Wil.

The sleeping figure began to stir. Quickly, Mongo grabbed the comforter, whipped it back, and struck with full force at the head. Amid the screams of men and a snarling demon came the cracking of bone; it was midway through the third blow that he saw the long, silver-gray strands of desheveled hair and realized that his cleaver had caved in the unfamiliar face of a woman. The bed became an inferno as covers flew up and Ellem sprang out.

"What in tarnation! What's goin' on here? What? Lawdy, Lawdy!" he yelled, springing from the bed. Utterly confused, Mongo froze.

Wil, with some difficulty, managed to slaughter the animal, and now had Ellem corralled in the one corner. In his long nightgown he resembled a stringed puppet trying to fly, flapping his arms, running to the right, then to the left, as Wil kept cutting off his escape.

"Get him, get him!" Wil yelled. Suddenly, Mongo was alive. Screaming in Ashantee, he leaped onto the bed and into the air. His first blow missed. The second caught Ellem in the neck. He slashed once more, and when he straightened up, he was holding Ellem's blood-covered head by the long, black hairs. Abruptly, the room was alive with light and people, who stood in the doorway open-mouthed at the bloody drama. Wil drove into the crowd, slashing with his knife, and it melted before him. With Mongo in his wake, he slashed his way down the narrow corridor amid the screams and curses of people pushed back on top of one another. One man foolishly tried to grab Mongo's cleaver and got his arm opened to the bone at the elbow. He fell to his knees and tried to stop the blood that gushed from an artery and splashed on the white wall making odd patterns as it ran down and over the baseboard.

Suddenly, both slaves were out in the cool night air headed toward the horses tied in the woods behind the barn. Just before they reached the barn, Solomon and Charlie came running around a corner of the barn with drawn pistols, cutting them off. Abruptly, the runners changed direction. They were halfway down the line of cabins before the first shots splattered into the cabins around them.

Chapter Sixteen

The first streaks of light of a new day were breaking through the dense woods as the two tired runners stumbled into the swamp. The stench of the brackish water made them take short breaths, and the noise of their splashing alarmed the swamp's inhabitants, who screamed back in anger and fear.

Because of dense sawgrass that cut their faces and hands, it took two hours to travel a half mile. When they had gotten through it and to a slight rise, they flopped down in a patch of sunshine that miraculously cut through the dense growth. For a long moment they held their breath and listened. Mongo said, "Ah don't hear nothin'. How 'bout you?"

" 'Nothin'," Wil answered. "Ain't that just fine! Haw, haw," he laughed loudly.

"Hush that loud talkin'," Mongo snapped. In spite of the warm sun both men shivered. They waited a little longer, listening for the sounds they knew had to come sooner or later. Then they were back in the water, laboriously struggling through the muck.

The horses and supplies left behind had Mongo worried. It would go hard on them. And he hadn't counted on getting through a swamp. He would have to rely solely on Wil's skills.

"You know for sure we headed, right?"

"Don't know nothin' for sure," Wil snickered over his shoulder. Mongo fingered the cleaver under his belt.

"Don't you be wise with me, boy," Mongo hissed. "Ah separate your head faster than lightnin' and leave you for the 'gators to chaw on."

"We goin' okay," Wil said solemnly.

The water became covered with thick algae scum that the water moccasins made trails through as they slithered before them, while mosquitoes large as flies attacked without letup. Still, they pushed on, forcing their legs through the sucking mud and watching for the snakes and 'gators until, at dusk, hungry and with every bone aching, they found dry ground and dropped to rest for the night.

Mongo lay on his back and studied the moonlight slicing through the long strands of Spanish moss that hung from the cypress trees. They had been going for almost twenty-four hours. His mouth tasted of acid, and his body ached everywhere, but he was alive and free! In a short time sleep came, and he began to float through a beautiful country. In the distance he saw Martha dance and gesture to him. Then Martha was gone, and he saw Tilah and the boys sitting in the doorway of their hut. He called to them, but they did not look up. When he drew closer to them, he saw they were dead.

Sound brought him abruptly back to reality. He sat up and listened. He heard it again, far away, the mournful yelp of a bloodhound. He shivered. Wil was asleep.

"Wil, wake up," Mongo whispered, shaking Wil violently.

Wil sat up all at once. "What's happenin', what's happenin'?"

"Listen."

For a long moment they listened. Then they heard the hound cries, several of them, growing louder.

"What we do?" Wil whispered.

"They won't come in the swamp at night," Mongo said.

Mongo's prediction was correct. The shrill bays of the hounds moved around them on the outskirts of the swamp. Neither slept any more that night. They huddled in the chilly damp air, hugging their knees to keep warm, and listened to the maddening sound of the hounds frantically trying to pick up their scent. At dawn they were in the water.

For two more days they kept moving southward, and the hounds' cries never were far away. It was at dusk of the fourth day that Wil dropped to the ground holding his stomach. He fell into a feverish sleep. Soon Mongo slept, too. It was hours later when they were shocked awake by a gunshot to the west. They never went back to sleep. In the morning Mongo saw that Wil was very weak. The big man lay with his mouth open, breathing in pants and burning with fever. In spite of his hate, a twinge of compassion flitted through him.

"You got the fire, huh?"

"Yeah, bad."

Mongo turned it over and over, but he could not make a decision. He waded into the cool water.

"You leavin' ol' Wil?"

"You stay put. Be back." He started moving away.

"You goin' turn us in?" Wil yelled hoarsely after him.

"Naw, ah figure out somethin', but you stay put, you

hear?" Mongo proceeded through the swamp, searching for particular herbs he knew were effective for fever. Soon he found himself in underbush so thick he could hardly penetrate it. Thorns ripped his skin and finally forced him to backtrack. He went a long way around the thicket, but then got lost. He wandered around most of the day, unable to tell direction because the sun was hidden by thick foliage. He had stopped to rest when, suddenly, a tortured scream erupted to his left, followed by a gunshot. They had found Wil.

Panicky, he plunged into the swamp. When night came, he found dry ground and fell down exhausted.

When he awoke at dawn, he was very weak and burning up with fever. He needed food. He saw a frog but failed to catch it. For the first time, he realized that he might not make it, that he might die in this swamp so far from home. A dread he had never known filled him. The pride that had gotten him through hard times in the past seemed inadequate now. He was crawling aimlessly, like a maimed animal, when, quite unexpectedly, he came to a little meadow with open blue sky and bright sunshine.

He stayed there the rest of the day, digging in the soil for grubs. He dug around a rotted tree and found a salamander, which he ate. He lay in the grass on his back and let the sun bore into his body and tried to forget the pain that kept stabbing him. He slept a long time. When he awoke, it was night. The stars were shining intensely. He searched the southern sky and found his favorite figure, the hunter, with the three stars at his waist and the two bright ones at each shoulder. Somehow his discovery comforted him. At once he was a boy sitting with his father before their fire.

"How did the warrior come to be?"

"He always was, son."

"But how . . . ?"

"Shhh. You are too young to worry about such things." Was it all pretense? The religious ritual performed because it was expected? Father, so wise and honest in all things, even about gods. But why didn't he know about the warrior?

He lay there in high fever, drifting in and out of reality. Thinking crazy things. He was sure he heard war drums and the cries of little children from somewhere in the swamp. Then he heard the rhythmic clanging of heavy chains so clearly that he forced himself on one elbow to determine the direction of the sound. He lay back down and looked again for the warrior. If he could only hold onto the warrior, he might make it. As he concentrated on the brilliant sky, questions he had as a young man gnawed at him. He saw a truth. When man is desperate, his searching becomes honest.

His desperation prompted him to pray. But to which god? What could he pray? The question was: was there a God? He knew there were idols that his people created and worshipped. He listened to the many night voices of the swamp, and a great desire to live permeated him. He fought it awhile, then whispered, "Great warrior, don't let Mongo die in this swamp like this. Let him die fightin' like an Ashantee."

The stars were so magnificent and orderly. Each had a place and never varied one from another, and that made him think of Tilah's mats. Multi-colored and beautifully woven they were, though he had never told her that. He wished now he had. He wished now he had done a lot of things. The stars had harmony and pattern and a reason for being, just as every color in Tilah's mat did. If design is there in the mats, in the stars, then there must be a designer, he reasoned. He turned it over and over, savoring, testing, making sure of his logic. He thought about the rhythm and balance in nature he had always taken for granted. He remembered when his first son was born, what a miracle it had seemed to him. How quickly he had forgotten. Now many memories flooded into his mind, substantiating that just as Tilah's mats did not happen by accident, neither did the warrior in the sky. But who caused it all? The gods of his father? Not likely. They weren't big enough. Martha's Jesus? Somehow, he didn't seem big enough, either. He wished he had paid closer attention to Martha's teaching.

An awful presence brushed him and made him cringe. He began to lose consciousness again and fought it once more. A new thought flitted in the deep recesses of his mind, and it seemed important that he capture it. Then it blossomed out and awed him. It was that as long as he remained proud and relied on his own powers, he would never know the answer to the riddle of the warrior.

He mulled over this, trying to understand while the black clouds continued to form, threatening him. He knew he was losing. Something deep within urged him to cry out for help, but he tightened up and would not.

Ah, but he would give anything for the touch of a human being. Tilah. Doctor Sam. Martha. He relived, in a moment, each one's touch, each one's tenderness. He wondered if he hated Martha's Jesus because it made her and the others so subservient. How he hated that quality in his people, especially the Christians! If a black man had to lick a white man's feet when he became a

Christian, that was not for him!

Then he remembered how Gabriel had stepped out of the line to face Ellem, and he had to admit that was the bravest thing he had ever known a man to do. Gabe had done that even for those he knew hated him for his faith. Many times he had wondered where Gabe had gotten his power. It went beyond self-respect or even pride. Was it love? He suspected that love had done some impossible things in his life. Oh, how forsaken and love-barren he felt! If only he could love once more, he would know how to receive . . . and how to give . . .

His thoughts became jumbled, and he saw the caved-in face of the light-haired lady of Ellem's bed float through the swamp. He almost yelled out in fright, but then she was gone. He remembered the ancient tribal belief about the shedding of innocent blood, and he feared avenging spirits. How could he have made such a great error? Now he began to relive the secret things of his life that made him feel ashamed. He saw the hypocrisy, the pretense, the arrogance. He remembered bitterly how he had refused to believe that Tilah hadn't willingly given herself to the Captain, and now he saw that it was because of the moral twist in his own life. He saw himself as a pathetic creature who had gloried in fame and respect for their sake alone, who sought to satisfy self first, having hardly any love or goodness at all. He saw it all in a moment, and he hated it, but he knew it was the truth. Suddenly, he didn't feel he had any right to be proud at all.

And then, he broke. He began to sob . . . long, wailing sobs from his soul. For a long time after, he lay quietly, vowing that if he lived, he would make a lot of things right. Love, he thought, I have seen you in a trusting little child and in the tender hands of a grown man. I have seen your magic, been touched by your power, but I have never known you. I wish to know you. I would give anything to know you.

A question came to him: *would you give your life?*

This time, when the black clouds threatened, he had no strength left. His last conscious effort before he was smothered was, "Oh, God. God that made the warrior . . . I give you my life."

He was on a blazing white beach where giant ostriches strutted, where brilliantly arrayed flowers bloomed living rainbow colors and the sunset left one breathless. He saw, too, the lowlands purple in the morning mist, of vines and the giant northern mountains where big-horned ibex and bearded aoudad tiptoed over the crevices. He tasted the cold water that came down from the mountains, and he took it all in with much longing, as though this would be the last time he would pass this way.

Chapter Seventeen

"Wake up, Nigger." The sharp jab in his chest exploded him awake. "Ah said, wake up, Nigger." He opened his eyes and was blinded by the brightness. Then he saw the muzzle of the rifle six inches from his face. The face at the other end was lost in the sun. "On your feet, boy." Once again the rifle dug painfully into his chest.

Mongo rolled on his side and got one leg under himself. When the man saw that he was having trouble, he didn't help but waited till Mongo eventually found his feet.

"We been lookin' high and low for you, boy. Half the state ain't slept in a week. You sure 'nough a bigun. What they call you, Mongo?"

"Huh?" Mongo played dumb.

"You heard me," the man said through narrowed eyes. He was young and very lean, and he chewed his tobacco nervously. The trigger finger on the Enfield rifle was white from pressure. Mongo gambled.

"Name's Luke. Come out to the swamp huntin' razor backs. Got maself lost. Been here with hardly nothin' to eat, near died."

"Your name ain't Mongo?"

"No sir. Name's Luke." Then anticipating the man's next question, he said, "Got ma freedom papers three years ago from over in Georgia. Good master."

"Let's see them papers, *Luke*."

Mongo shook his head and scratched it dumb-like as he had seen other blacks do to avoid an issue. "Lost them freedom papers a year ago. Ah knowed ah get a peck of troublement for that. Crossin' a stream and off they floats." He stood looking down at the ground like he was supposed to, waiting for a white man's judgment. He was very thirsty.

"Does you have water?" he asked. The man took a leather flask from his hip and handed it to him, cautiously. "Don't tech that bottle, Nigger." Mongo knew what he meant and drank from the flask held away from his lips. The water was cool and sweet, not like the rancid swamp water. He was careful to leave some.

"You do appear tuckered," the man said. He studied Mongo a moment; then, transferring the Enfield rifle to his left hand, he reached into a small canvas bag at his feet and pulled out a wax paper packet. He tossed it to Mongo. "Cain't stand to see a man hungry, even a nigger. Set down and chaw on this."

Mongo sat down under a tree and carefully untied the packet. "Ah thanks you kindly."

The packet contained two fried chicken legs and three slices of corn bread. He chewed the food gratefully, savoring, licking, not letting one crumb fall to the ground. When he was done, he sat back and closed his eyes, enjoying the warm sun in his face. His sickness was gone; his mind was perfectly clear. He had never been so grateful for life as he was at that moment. He felt a mellowness, too, which was new to him, and he realized he wasn't afraid. Abruptly, he saw that fear had driven him most of his life. He thought about the nervous young man and wondered if the man was afraid of him.

He remembered the events of last night and was sure God had given his life back to him. But what of this man with his nervous eyes and obvious distrust? Was he also an answer, somehow? The man could end his life at any moment; yet he wasn't his enemy. An enemy was someone you hated.

"Them victuals real scrumptious. Ah thank you kindly." Mongo smiled.

"Huh," the man grunted. He fumbled for a fresh wad of tobacco.

Mongo closed his eyes again and hummed a song the slaves sang frequently in the fields when they were in a happy mood. He felt so good. He didn't quite understand it, but he knew his life would never be the same. After a moment he said, "Can ah ask you somethin'?"

"Sure."

"You a planter man?"

"Yep, ah got me a little place up aways."

"Does you have slaves?"

"Two. Cain't 'ford any more."

"You beats 'em?"

"Would iffen ah had to. Ain't had to, yet."

"That's good."

"Looks like you been handled some," the man snickered. Mongo's hand went up to the scar on his forehead. "More than ah like to recollect."

"Thought you said you had a good master."

"Last one fine, fine. Man before that, not so fine," Mongo lied.

Neither spoke for awhile, and Mongo's last words kept repeating themselves in his head. It bothered him greatly that he had lied. "Well, ah'm ready," the man announced. "You get yourself together."

Mongo took a deep breath. "Where we goin'?"

"Ah'm takin' you back with me. We find out who you is. You tellin' the truth, you won't have no cause to fret. Ah sees to that. Lay down on your belly and put your hands behind you."

Mongo did as ordered. The man took a length of rope from his sack and, putting a knee on Mongo's back, tied his hands tightly. Then he made a loop in the rope and tied it securely around Mongo's neck. Taking the end, he stepped back about ten feet and said, "Git up, easy."

Awkwardly, Mongo got to his feet.

"You start out that aways. 'Member, ah'm right behind you, and ah warn you now. That bounty notice don't say nothin' 'bout you bein' alive."

The ground over which they traveled was thick with brush. By late afternoon they had not gotten far. Just before dusk they moved out of the bottom and started up a heavily wooded slope. When they came to a fallen oak, the man stopped and said, "Best we stop here for the night."

The man tied Mongo to a tree, leaving his right hand free, and began to scrounge for fire wood. He built the fire at the base of a large boulder. The air had turned crisp, and when the man moved Mongo to a tree closer to the fire, he was grateful. He was grateful, too, that the Enfield no longer pointed at him, but was resting across the lap of its owner who was now rummaging in his bag.

"Good thing Myra packed all this grub. Ah'd be in a

fix," he muttered half to himself. "Reckon you ain't too picky." He took the first packet he found and threw it to Mongo. Mongo opened the packet, using his teeth and free hand. This time he fared with a bacon sandwich and an apple which he ate, core and all. Meanwhile, his captor was making coffee in an old pot he had removed from his pack. He set the pot in the fire and found a tin cup. When the coffee was ready, he filled the cup for Mongo and put it down where he could reach it. When he saw Mongo hesitate before drinking, he said, "Ah 'spose you can drink it. Man can't drink hot coffee 'cept only one way. Ah wash it out good when you're done."

The coffee was invigorating, and Mongo humbly asked for a second cup.

"You don't appear such an 'onery cuss, least not one'd kill three men," the man said while he poured the coffee.

"Three men?"

"Yep, that's what the story is. Runaway called Mongo butchered two men and a woman with a cleaver."

Mongo shook his head slowly, unbelievingly. He wondered who the other man was or if the story merely had grown from the telling. Perhaps it was the one who tried to grab Wil in the hallway.

"Sure caused an uproar. Ever' toad can hold a squirrel rifle is out lookin'. Even some militia men. Found one of the runaways night before last. He tried to run, but he didn't get far."

"Mi-lit-ia?"

"Yep, soldier boys from Orleans. They everwhere these days. Gettin' ready to fight the North."

"Why they gonna' fight?"

"Don't know no better, ah guess," the man mused.

But he saw Mongo wasn't satisfied with his answer.

"Well, this here thing's been buildin' to blow out for a spell now. Them Northerners tryin' to tell these big planters they can't own slaves when everybody knows they was the first to have 'em and they're just jealous of all this here money bein' made now 'cause of slave labor. Don't none of it make no sense. Ah just stays out of it. What do ah know? Ah do declare, though, this Lincoln feller's got some good points. This Union splits, we might never get together again. Me, ah'm for the Union. 'Course ah ain't got no big plantation, neither."

"Lin-coln," Mongo said thoughtfully, trying to remember where he had heard the name. Martha. It had something to do with her. Then he remembered. That night at the prayer meeting. The preacher man had talked about a Christian in the north named Lincoln who was sympathetic to the slaves. Mongo felt a twinge of excitement.

"Yeah, Lincoln. Heard of him? Should have. Him and his Republicans."

"His people called which?"

"Republicans."

"Re-pub-li-cans?" Mongo answered. He wanted to remember that.

When the fire began to die, the man threw on more wood; and each became absorbed in watching the sparks spit out from the dried limbs. For a while neither spoke. Mongo liked the man. It was obvious that a gentle nature lay beneath the gruff exterior.

"Can ah ask you somethin'?" he said.

"Fire away."

"What's your name?"

"Elmer. Elmer Kinkle."

"Elmer Kin-kle." Mongo mused. The sound of it tickled him. "Ah sure 'nough like that," he smiled. "Can ah ask you somethin' else?"

"Sure 'nough."

"Does you have a wife and younguns?"

"Wife, no younguns, though," Elmer said quietly. Mongo wondered if he should ask the next question.

"How come no younguns?"

Elmer hesitated. "We can't have none."

Mongo tried to think of something appropriate to say. Then he said, "One of these days you find a little ninnie somebody don't want, and you take him in for your own. Betcha!"

"Don't reckon."

"How come?"

"Wife's not able to take care of a youngun'." When Elmer saw Mongo was confused, he said, "Ah ain't told too many, but ah'll tell you. How 'bout another cup?"

Mongo smiled assent. The steaming coffee seemed to sit just right with him; and as he settled back against the tree in anticipation of Elmer's story, he realized that even though this man was white and was his captor, he cared about him. He couldn't get over how joyful he felt, and free from care, even though he knew that quite possibly he could be hanging by his thumbs in a fortnight. He looked up and saw a full moon emerge from a cloud. And he saw the stars, so vivid through the trees; and he remembered the warrior.

"We was comin' home from town late one night, Myra and me," Elmer began, taking out a hand-carved pipe from his leather vest and filling it. "We was in a buckboard, and ah was drivin' a pair of mules ah had just traded some heifers for a week before. Them mules was real peppy. They'd run for no excuse. And fast? Ooohie! And sure-footed? Man, them mules could haul timber over trails you couldn't walk over. Now that's the truth. Ah was sure proud of 'em. Best trade ah ever made. Well, anyway, we'd been out, Myra and me, seein' some other newlyweds in town. See, ah been married five years; and this happened six months after we got hitched." He paused to relight the pipe with the branch from the fire. "Now, ah don't want you to get the idea ah'm no town drunk, 'cause ah ain't. Ah liked a little nip once in a while. Myra never approved, but she never said much about it. Ah use to get her to try it, to get her to be more fun; so she'd take a toddy just make me happy, but ah knew she hated it.

"Well, anyways, ol' Marvin . . . that's ma buddy who just got hisself hitched to this little filly . . . wants to celebrate by trying corn liquor he's been easin' along; and first thing ah knew we got ourselves skunk drunk. When Myra found us, she 'bout throw'd a fit.

"Well, we started out for home; and ah got them mules a fast-steppin', kinda showin' em off, you know, for Myra? She said nary a word; she was still mad. Ah don't know what got into me, but she wouldn't give me no satisfaction. Ah cussed and licked them mules, and they took off like demons was on 'em. Myra was screamin' for me to stop, but ah 'magine ah run them mules three miles fast as they would go.

"There's a creek runs across the road just below ma place that's dry most of the year. The road curves at that point and gets rough. Ah know'd we was comin' to it, but that's all ah knew. Ah didn't even know it when she fell out . . . she . . ."

Elmer broke. It was some time before he continued.

"The last thing in the world ah ever wanted to happen was for her to get hurt. Ah'd give ma life iffen she could use them legs again. Ah wait on her hand and foot today. Do anything to make her life better. Ah loves her. Oh, she forgive me all right. Ah ran back down that road lookin' for her screamin' like a mad man, and when ah found her, ah held her in ma arms and pleaded with her to forgive me. And she just looked at me and smiled that smile of hers. Ah carried her twisted body to the house and went for help. Her back was broken." Elmer sat looking down at the ground. Mongo felt his grief.

"Ma life took a turn then. Ah never touched a drop after that night. You might say ah did a lot of growin' up all at once."

'Can ah ask you somethin'?" asked Mongo.

"Sure thing."

"How come you out here?"

"The bounty."

"That's all?"

"That's all. Five hundred dollars. Ah got the notion that iffen ah got lucky, ah'd use the money to hire one of them specialists up north for Myra. Doctor Bass said there might be a chance she can walk someday with an operation."

"Did you say, 'Dr. Bass'?" Mongo asked. "Man with one eye?"

"Sure 'nough. You know him?"

"Heard his name on the plantation," Mongo lied. "Was he 'round here?"

"Yep. Had a place about forty miles north of here. Good man. Had time for everyone, no matter how poor you was. Had a good practice. Folks hated to see him leave. But a man's got to do what he thinks is right."

"Where'd he go?" Mongo asked.

"Oh, last I heard he was up around Illinois. He got interested in politics. Use to travel to them big conventions. Got chummy with them politicians. He was a fighter, all right. Always arguing 'bout how wrong slave holdin' was. I guess, when he was younger he had some bad experiences. Never talked about that part of his life. Guess he figured he could do more good up north with Lincoln's people. Never will forget what he said to me the day he left."

"What's that?"

"Well, it's kinda personal; but I guess it won't hurt to say it. Its just that he made me see that ah wanted Myra healed, sure 'nough, but more 'cause ah wanted a whole woman. Ah mean, we hadn't ever slept together since the accident. You know what ah mean? Dr. Bass, he said that I'd have to change my way of thinkin'. You know what ah mean?"

"Reckon so."

"Yes, but it ain't right. Ah've even hankered to pester a wilder woman who's been eyein' me in town. Sometimes ah get such thoughts ah think ah'm possessed, ah swore. Ah want to do the right thing, but ah just cain't. Why am ah tellin' you all this?"

"Ah knows what you sayin'," Mongo said. "There things ah'm ashamed of, a whole lifetime of things." Mongo looked out into the night. "But ah aims to change. Ah made a promise last night, an ah aims to keep it."

"Who'd you promise?"

"God," Mongo said, hesitantly.

"You kiddin' me?"

"No sir. Ah prayed last night to God; and somethin' come over me today, ah swore. Ah got joy in me where ah had hate. Don't reckon you believes me, but it's the truth. Ain't had nothin' like this happen before."

Elmer gazed absent-mindedly at the fire which was beginning to die. "Ah knows what you mean. Man gets religion, his whole outlook changes. Happen to me once."

"Sure 'nough?"

"That's right. Seem like a long time ago, though it weren't. Happened at a camp meetin' one night. That preacher was talkin' right at me; and when he asked folks to come and get saved, ah went up there. And when ah prayed that salvation prayer, ah had such a feelin' of joy go through me, why, it gives me the shivers still just to tell it. A month later it was all gone. Ah lived in a home where there was bickering and pickin' all day long, no love at all. The old man would carry a Bible in one hand and a stick to lick you with in the other. After a while ah got sick of gettin' licked and their kind of Christianity that was just a set of rules and nothin' else. Ah fell in with a bad bunch then, but ah can't blame nobody for that. No one made me go out and drink maself blind. Yep, ah sure made a mess of ma life." Elmer shook his head dejectedly.

"Maybe you can patch it up. It ain't too late," Mongo said, smiling.

"Ah dunno. Ah just don't know."

It was getting late. A fog was coming up from the bottom, and the two men prepared to turn in. Elmer apologized as he tied Mongo's right hand behind him again, and he put the canvas bag under Mongo's head for a pillow. Mongo was touched by the gesture. He fought with it till he could not contain himself any longer. He watched Elmer build up the fire, then lay down facing him with the rifle beside him.

"Say a . . ."

"Yep."

"Ah just didn't want to hold it from you no more. Ma name ain't Luke."

"Ah know'd right along."

"How come you know?"

"They said you ain't no ordinary nigger. Ah sees what they mean. You know, we been raised to believe we bettern' youens'. But ah never met no nigger like you before."

"They lots 'round. They's 'fraid that's all. They need love an 'couragement. And they need to find God, too."

"Reckon," Elmer said.

Long after Elmer's snoring began, Mongo lay awake staring at the stars and the full moon that silhouetted the fleecy cirrus clouds. He remembered how the Reverend had stressed that night at the prayer meeting how Lincoln was fighting against slavery. Now there was talk of war. Was the whole South rising up against Lincoln and his Republicans? Did the blacks know? Where they rallying even now or scheming and preparing for an uprising in the future? There had been no talk on the plantation, but little wonder. Such news would have been suppressed. And other plantations? Undoubtedly, the same was true. And what of Doctor Bass? Was he helping Lincoln free the slaves? He would give anything to be free to travel north and help in the fight to end suffering.

His body began to move uneasily on his bed of leaves. He tried to think what Lincoln might look like.

At first he imagined a big man, very powerful. Then he changed his mind and decided that he was slight and used his mind to fight. And what of the Republicans? What kind of men were they? Try as he might, he could not sleep. It was nagging him, this thing that all over the South blacks did not know that a war was coming. He knew all about war. He knew, too, that there had to be thousands of his people whose spirits had not been broken, who could be led to help in the fight for their freedom.

Slowly his wrists began to rotate in the ropes, until he was tugging and twisting; but his efforts were wasted. He lay quietly for a while, till a strong thought came to him that there was a better way than what he was planning. Then he remembered his commitment to the God of the warrior. He had given Him his life only to have it handed right back again. There had to be a reason.

It wasn't long before he was straining at the ropes again. Finally, he lay sopping wet and exhausted with his face in the dirt, and for the second time in two days, with no other recourse, he rolled over, turned his face to the sky, and surrendered his will. A short while later he was sleeping peacefully.

Elmer nudged him awake at sunup. His arms and shoulders ached from the awkward position he had slept in, and he shivered till Elmer got the fire going. They had some beans and more strong coffee, and soon they were trudging to the top of the ridge. They stopped at the crest and gazed into a valley in which cattle grazed peacefully in lush dew-covered meadows. Across from them stood another timber ridge about as high as the one on which they stood. "See that there ridge yonder?"

"Yes sir."

"When we get to that one, we'll see the river."

"Ol' Miss?"

"Yep."

They moved down the slope with Elmer lying back, keeping the rope tight between them. At high noon they stopped halfway across the valley, sat in the shade of a honeysuckle, and munched on cornbread and apples. Mongo was intrigued with the fertile valley and began to tell Elmer of the richness of his own country. At Elmer's urging he told how he had been captured, about the slave ship, and how Ellem had bought him in New Orleans. When he spoke of Ellem's brutality, he noticed Elmer grimace and mutter under his breath. They moved out then across the valley and up the steep slope. An hour before dusk they made the top of the second ridge; and as far as they could see in either direction, lay the Mississippi. Smoke spiraled from tiny houses on the other side, and a riverboat opposite them paddled her way upstream.

"See that small hill over to the right near hat point on the river?" Elmer asked.

"Yes sir."

"Ma place right behind that hill. And beyond that's Orleans."

"Sure 'nough?"

"Sure 'nough."

"The north is that way?" Mongo asked, pointing to his left, though he knew the answer.

"That's right," Elmer said.

They went back down the ridge a way and found a good place to camp for the night. After they were settled and munching on the last of Elmer's beans, Elmer leaned back against a tree stump and said, "You know, man's been through what you have should be full of hate and poison, but you ain't. Lots of white folks could take a lesson from you." He paused, trying to construct his next thoughts. "Ah don't know what really happened at Ellem's place, but his niggerbustin' ways weren't no secret. Far's ah'm concerned he got his just desserts. There's too much hate in this country. Ah seen men turn into animals over the profits to be made because of slavery. From what ah hear, the richer Ellem got, the meaner he got. Well, someone's got to stand up. I had thought to take you to Orleans where you'd have half a chance. Them planters around Ellem's say they goin' to take you apart, piece by piece, when they catch you. But now I'm thinkin' you got no chance in Orleans, neither. Ah guess what ah'm tryin' to say is ah takes ma hat off to you; and ah ain't never said that to a man before, 'specially a black man."

Mongo opened his mouth, but the words could not come. Instead, tears came; so he put his head down on his drawn-up knees and said nothing.

For a long time it was quiet. Then Elmer said, "Just do me one favor. Don't ever breathe a word 'bout us bein' together."

Mongo looked up quickly when he got the meaning of Elmer's words. And as he studied Elmer's face, he made the second vow of his life—that somehow, someday he would help this man gather the money for his wife's operation.

They turned in, and both slept better than they had in a long time. It was daylight when Mongo opened his eyes and found a bowie knife lying nearby with the almost empty canvas bag of victuals. Elmer was gone.

Mongo cut his ropes, snatched up the sack, and climbed quickly to the top of the ridge. There was no sign of life. Excitement flooded him as he realized he was free. As he stood looking down at the mammoth river, he was tempted to continue to New Orleans where the ships lay at anchor; but the wind that smelled faintly of the ocean caressing his cheek carried the cries of souls dying of suffocation in a hundred slaver holds. He knew that no matter what his personal desires, he could make only one decision. Just to make sure, he looked skyward and said aloud, "Is this what you want?" Slowly he turned to the north and saw the river recede into a thin ribbon. New courage welled up within him, and he knew the answer. The men he must find were a long way up that river. He began to walk along the crest of the ridge.

He moved steadily hour after hour and stopped only once to treat himself to a slice of corn bread. The ridge finally began to slope downward to a point that ran a mile out into the river. It was dusk when he made the bank and stuck his toes into the water heavy with sediment. He was surprised at the swift current. He found a place in the thicket not too far away where he felt safe. He slept fitfully and awoke at midnight; and because of the bright moon, he decided to travel at once. From that night on, Mongo carefully followed his plan of sleeping all day and traveling only by night. He built no fires and ate sparingly of his rations. When they were gone, he used a fish hook and line he found on the shore one morning; and using night crawlers, he caught catfish which he ate raw. As his eyes adjusted to night, he learned to recognize ditches, tree limbs, or fences. He became expert, too, at stealing chickens and cleaning them by moonlight. When he could, he stayed close to the river, and sometimes had to hand-feel his way through a thick stand of timber or other obstacles.

During the second week, he narrowly missed getting caught. Unwittingly, he had made his bed near a water path. He was awakened by voices and looked into the face of a pretty young black with a clay pot on her head. The half dozen other girls and driver had not seen him. Mongo put his finger to his lips, and she smiled and was gone. He didn't wait to learn if she told the others.

He knew his journey would be long, but he was not concerned. He knew that if he averaged a good amount each night, the nights would add up and his journey would end. His new peace allowed him to live each day, one day at a time. He refused to worry about obstacles before he met them. For the first time in his life, he had a cause, a purpose to his life, a zest that would not die. He thought about Lincoln and his Republicans incessantly and found himself praying for them as he lay looking up at the stars before starting another night's journey. He didn't bother to keep track of the weeks or even the months, but one night he came to a large city. From his hiding place he saw troops boarding huge paddlewheel boats. He was awed that there were so many, all looking exactly alike. When it grew dark and Memphis' lights flickered on one by one, he tarried a long while and marveled at the city that had become full of stars.

When his clothes wore out, he stole some overalls and a denim shirt from a clothesline, and though he tried to rationalize the theft by his need, he was troubled by the thieving he had to do to keep going. He determined after that not to steal even if he starved to death.

As the warmer weather melted the snows of the

north, the Mississippi swelled and a new danger threatened: floods. One night he came upon hundreds of blacks, their bare backs gleaming in the light of lanterns as they struggled to hold back a break in a levee with sand bags. The overseers whipped them constantly. Mongo made a wide detour, trying not to let their brutality ignite old familiar feelings of bitterness.

He had been wading in flood water up to his waist for the greater part of a week, and with no fire to dry off with, he became ill with a high fever. He lay for days coughing in a hayloft of an abandoned barn, wrapped in an old horse blanket he found in the loft. He caught pigeons roosting in the rafters to keep alive, till a black man and his woman, who had determined to make "freedom land" but had tired of the journey and now lived in a humble shack near the barn, found him. Mongo learned from them that the war had begun, and the blacks in those parts had not rallied. This news discouraged Mongo, and though he wanted to press on, he lived with the couple till he was stronger. One warm night about a month later, the man came home drunk and offered Mongo his woman for the night. Mongo offered him God in return. The man threw him out, and Mongo continued his journey.

Chapter Eighteen

Gordy, Augie, and Eli begged, kicked, and shouted drunkenly at their mule, who didn't like carrying three men—and grudgingly picked her way down the steep trail to the river. Gordy, age 24, held the reins. He was tall, willowy, and scarred from much brawling; when the mule would try to use a tree to scrape them off, he would sink his teeth into into her ear. Augie, four years younger, did most of the kicking and yelling. Eli, his younger brother, eighteen and slow-witted, was content to hold the mule's tail with one hand and the bottle of "red eye" with the other.

When they got to the river, they tied the mule in a thicket and went to their favorite hiding place, a cove. Gordy was the first in and saw that the fishing poles were gone. He grabbed Augie and, towering over him, shouted in his face, "Did ya put them poles outta sight like ah said?"

"Yeah, I did, I did," Augie said. He pulled away and went over to the hollowed-out tree.

"He put 'em there in the tree. I seen him do it," Eli announced. "I sure did."

"That ain't sayin' much," Gordy said, disgustedly. He loved to fish. He grabbed the bottle roughly from Eli and sat down on a log on which obscene words and pictures were carved. The two followed his example and waited for him to relinquish the bottle. Augie drank next, only he tried to take a longer swig than Gordy had. When Eli took the bottle he held it exactly like Augie, but he only took a little swig.

Though it was only May, it threatened to be a very warm day. Gordy stretched out, preparing for a snooze. Eli whispered to his brother, "Why do we have to come down here, Aug? There ain't never nothin' to do."

"This is conscript day, dummy. You want them tin soldiers catch ya and make ya march all day in the hot sun and fight and never let ya do what ya want?"

"No," Eli agreed. "But can't we do sumpthin' 'sides sit around?"

Augie didn't answer.

"Hey," Eli said excitedly, "let's go find some frogs and pull their legs off."

"That ain't no fun," Augie mumbled lazily. The "red eye" was catching up.

Eli brooded. "You're an ol' stick-in-the-mud."

"Shut up."

Eli sat quietly for as long as he could. Then he said, "Aug?"

"Huh?"

"Kin I go look for stuff?"

"Yeah. Don't fall in. If you see anyone, come back."

Elated now, Eli jumped up and walked along the shore. Five minutes later he came scampering back and shook Augie, who was almost asleep.

"Hey Aug, wake up, wake up." Both Gordy and Augie opened their eyes.

"What's the matter?" Gordy asked.

"There's a nigger layin' under our boat, and he's got our poles."

Gordy and Augie jumped to their feet. Eli took off ahead of them.

"Git back here, you half-wit," Gordy snapped. "You wanna give us away?" With Gordy in the lead they tip-toed around a bend to where a fair-sized river skiff lay bottom up in the weeds. Two black feet stuck out from under one end. Gordy directed the two to their positions and then picked up a thick tree limb. One of them flipped over the skiff, and all three pounced on the sleeping black underneath. Caught by surprise, Mongo struggled gamely to get free till Gordy's limb found its mark twice; and he slipped into unconsciousness. When he came to, he was tied hand and foot. He was jerked to his feet and stood blinking in the sun, his hair and beard full of grass husks, his clothes tattered. He was very thin.

"Where you from, Nigger?" Gordy asked.

"Down south, 'round Orleans," Mongo answered, looking Gordy in the eyes.

"What ya doin' way up here?" Augie asked. "You a runner?"

Mongo hesitated. He wanted to speak the truth, but was apprehensive.

"I'll bet he's a runner," Eli said, standing a little behind Augie.

"Maybe he's a spy," Eli repeated.

"You ain't answered my question, Nigger. I'm still waitin'."

Mongo cleared his throat, "Ah'm lookin' for a man," he said.

"I'll bet he is a spy," Augie said to Gordy.

"I'll bet he is too," said Eli.

Augie looked around for convicting evidence and saw the poles in the water.

"You took them poles, Nigger?" he asked.

"Ah borrowed 'em. Meant to put 'em away, when ah left," Mongo answered.

Gordy didn't believe him. "You stole them poles."

"No sir," Mongo answered, concerned now for the direction things were going.

"What's your name?" Augie asked.

"I'm doin' the interrogatin'." Gordy snapped.

"What's that?" Augie asked.

"Jest shut up." To Mongo, "What's your name?"

"Mongo," Mongo sighed, knowing what was coming.

"What's it mean?" Gordy asked.

"Means king," Mongo said quietly.

"King! Hey, we got ourselves a king," Augie laughed.

Gordy laughed, too, but became serious quickly. "What man you lookin' for?" he asked.

"Lincoln," Mongo answered.

"Abe Lincoln, the President?" Gordy asked, amazed.

"That's right," Mongo said quietly. They really laughed at that. Mongo waited.

"Wella, now tell me," Gordy asked, "what do you propose to do when you find Lincoln?"

"Try and bushwack him, I'll bet," Augie broke in.

"That right?" Gordy asked.

"No, sir."

"What then?" Gordy asked through narrowed eyes.

Mongo inhaled deeply. "Ah aims to help him free ma people."

There was a moment of unbelief, then howls once

again from the three. Mongo now began to analyze his chance for escape. Gordy breathlessly said, "If this don't take the cake! We got ourselves a thievin' nigger, probably a runaway, who thinks he's a king, and is gonna help the President free all the niggers. I don't believe it! Haw, haw."

"Folks 'round here don't think niggers should be free," Augie said.

"Yeah," Gordy agreed. "Especially crazy niggers."

For a moment it was quiet. Then Augie said, "Hey, Gord, you suppose he is crazy?"

"Dunno," Gordy said, pondering.

"Well, I think he's a reb spy, that's what I think," Eli said to get attention. They thought it over.

" 'Spossible," Gordy said.

"Naw, anything this half-wit thunk up can't be right," Augie mused. Eli fumed.

" 'Spossible," Gordy insisted.

"Well, we can find out easy 'nough," Augie said. "Let's make him confess."

It was a good idea, but Gordy didn't think of it. "Naw," he said. "Anybody knows niggers ain't smart enough for spyin'. You ever hear tell of the contrary?"

"Nope," Augie allowed.

"Now look a here, Nigger, you either crazy or a spy. But you gotta be one or the other." Gordy slobbered in Mongo's face. "Now which you gonna be? Take a pick . . .!"

Mongo licked his lips. "Ah'm neither," he said, quietly.

"Ah says diff'rent," Gordy insisted, pointing a finger in Mongo's face. "So don't contradict me. Now which are you?"

Mongo looked at the peacefully flowing river and

the gulls that kept swooping down and plucking their prey from the water. "Ah'm a man," he said, turning back to Gordy slowly, then staring him straight in the eye. Gordy never had a black look at him like that before. He didn't know what to make of it.

"You ain't neither," countered Augie. "You're a nigger, an old rag-tag of a crazy nigger." He stepped forward and savagely yanked Mongo's beard. He had never been able to grow a beard. For a brief instant fire roared inside Mongo.

"O.K., Mr. King, for the last time," Gordy said, "tell us what you're doin' 'round here."

Mongo spoke humbly. "Ah run away from the plantation. Ah heard tell 'bout Mister Lincoln, 'bout how he tryin' to help ma people. Ah comes to help him. That's all."

"That's all," Gordy mimicked. "That's all? You're a fool, Nigger. First of all, not everyone goes along with Lincoln on this freedom business. No one around here that I know of, anyway."

"I still say he's lyin', Gord," Augie said. "It's too farfetched."

"You know how far it is to Orleans?"

"No sir," Mongo answered.

"Twelve, maybe thirteen hundred miles. And you want us to believe you come up this river all the way to Quincy from Orleans, alone, without gettin' yourself caught?"

"Yes sir," Mongo said, soberly.

"Bull," sneered Gordy. "I don't know what you're doin' 'round here, but I don't believe you. You're a lyin', thievin' nigger that's got uppity ideas." Gordy was getting worked up now. "Let me ask you another question, King Nigger! When you get these niggers free, what do you propose to do with them?"

Mongo thought a moment. After a minute he said, "Help 'em believe in themselves, to hold their heads up 'cause they men, not animals. Help 'em to know God."

"God?" Augie jumped as though stung by a wasp. He was a preacher's kid who hated anything or anybody remotely religious. "You a Jesus man, besides?" he asked, incredulously.

Mongo pondered. "Does you mean, am ah a Christian?"

"Exactly," Augie sneered.

"Yes sir," Mongo answered after a moment.

"You been baptized?" Augie asked harshly.

"No sir," Mongo said, again hesitating.

"Then you ain't a Christian."

Mongo said nothing. Augie thought about it, then smiled. "Hey, don't fret none 'cause we can baptize you,"

Gordy looked quizzically at Augie. "What are you talkin' about?"

Augie was very serious now. "Man wants to be a Christian. I can baptize him 'cause my old man's a preacher, remember?" There were very few occasions when Augie knew more about a given subject than Gordy did, and he intended to make the most of it. He gathered himself up and in a pretentious tone and said, "Nigger, does you want to be baptized in the name of Jesus?"

The words were bringing back memories. There was a Sunday morning before one of Martha's church services, when the entire population went down to the pond and watched a visiting parson baptize several of Martha's pupils. He remembered how forcefully they had testified about their faith in Christ.

"Yes sir," he said, standing a little taller, "Jesus Christ is ma Master no matter what." He knew he wasn't helping himself. He was tempted to try to smooth-talk his way to freedom and continue the mission begun months earlier, to perhaps tell them of the large reward on his head which might gain him temporary safety. But he knew this was not the direction for him. He was greatly convicted to answer each question with complete honesty and not worry about consequences.

"No matter what, huh?" Augie sneered. "Ya sure about that?"

"Ah'm sure," he said, smiling; for now a new joy of much greater intensity and a love and understanding for the three flooded him.

"All right, we gonna' have ourselves a baptism ceremony. Right, Gord?"

"Sure, sure," Gordy answered.

They untied the rope from the boat and, making a noose in one end, put it around Mongo's chest. They led him along the river to where the water was deep and swift as it swept around a point.

"Now, this here's the procedure. No need for more than one of us getting' wet; so when you're ready, jump in and I'll say the proper words. I got the rope, so don't fret."

They stood very close behind him, but they were not untying his hands. When he didn't jump in, they shoved him into the cold water. Immediately, he was swept out to the full length of the rope. He began to paddlewheel with his legs and managed to keep his head just above water. Augie turned to Gordy, "Hey, I almost forgot. When a man is baptized, he is given a name. Got one in mind?"

"I dunno. Let's sit down here in the shade, have a nip, and think about it," Gordy answered. The three sat down and each took a swig from the bottle.

"What did he say his name was?" Gordy asked.

"King," Eli said quickly.

"Naa. Naa. The other one."

"Mongo," Augie said.

"Well, let's see, what goes with Mongo? Norm? Na. Everett?"

"Hey, how about Roy?" Eli asked.

They thought about it. Mongo's head was lower in the water as he began to tire. Gordy yelled out, "You still claim that story is true?" Mongo didn't speak.

"Say, I know," Augie said, "how about John? Mongo John."

"That's good," Gordy allowed. They had another round at the bottle. Mongo's head dipped below the water. When he came up, he was wide-eyed.

"Better get on with the ceremony, Preach," Gordy said, yawning, and they all laughed.

Augie slowly got to his feet, "Now sinner, ah wants you to pay special attention. Does you claim Jesus Christ as your Lord and Savior?"

Mongo was beginning to choke. "If you claim Jesus Christ as your Lord and Savior, by the authority of my old man, who is a preacher, I baptize you Mongo John in the name of the Father . . . and . . ."

Mongo was going under. "Hurry up, or your Christian ain't gonna be able to testify!" Gordy laughed.

" . . . of the Son . . . and the Holy Ghost . . ."

Mongo's face reappeared for the last time.

They sat there passing the bottle back and forth for a long time till it was empty, and all three lay down with their heads against a log. Soon Gordy was snoring loudly.

"Aug?" Eli whispered, hoarsely.
"Huh?"
"How could he do that?"
"Do what?" Augie mumbled.
"Die so easy."
"He was loco. Shut up, I wanna sleep."

Eli didn't say any more but lay there looking up at the swaying cottonwood directly overhead and listened to Gordy and Augie snoring discordantly. Then he got up and strolled back along the river to where the skiff was. He wasn't drunk anymore. He sat on one end of the skiff and dejectedly kicked at the pebbles of the shore with his bare feet. A tear rolled down his cheeks.

. . . .

"He was oppressed and he was afflicted, but yet he said never a word, he was brought as a lamb to the slaughter, and as a sheep before her shearers is dumb, so he stood silent before the ones condemning him."

(Isaiah 53:7)

Ron Rendleman

If you wish to communicate with the author, his address is:

Ron Rendleman
1070 Woodcliff
South Elgin, Ill. 60177